MATING SEASON

Dear Editor Book Three

EMILY SHARPE

Published by Blushing Books
An Imprint of
ABCD Graphics and Design, Inc.
A Virginia Corporation
977 Seminole Trail #233
Charlottesville, VA 22901

Emily Sharpe
Mating Season

eBook ISBN: 978-1-64563-706-6
Print ISBN: 978-1-64563-707-3
Audio ISBN: 978-1-64563-708-0
v1

Dedicated to the fine writers of Use Your Words writing group at the Inner Truth Project in Port St. Lucie, Florida, and in memory of my mother, who would have said a book like this should come in a brown paper bag.

Note from the Author

This is a work of fiction. Names, characters, businesses, events, and incidents are the products of the author's imagination. A few locations in *Mating Season* are real; others are made up. Resemblance to actual persons or events is purely coincidental, but the author sincerely hopes that all of us find the kind of love and happiness that is possible. *It's never too late!*

A New Beginning

Kristina Edwards stretched from her twelve-hour drive and twisted her long ponytail into a big knot, in preparation for the tough job ahead. What she really wanted was a hot shower, a glass of wine, and to sleep until noon the next day. *That's not happening,* she thought ruefully. *Way too much to do.*

As she opened the back of her SUV, she sighed. Even after a considerable amount of throwing out, giving away, and selling on Craigslist, the car was packed to the gills, as her sister Layla would say. She wished Layla could be there to help her unpack, but she had a relatively new baby to look after. Born prematurely, just before Christmas, her precious niece's name was fitting, Angela, their little angel. Still, Kristina missed the help. *That wasn't the best timing, big sister,* she thought wryly. As if anyone had foreseen this big a move.

She'd spent her Christmas break helping Layla and her husband Keith with the new baby. They had stopped just shy of actual prying, but they'd known something wasn't right with Kristina. She was different, both in personality and appearance. She hadn't told them, but the confusion and surprise in their faces when they saw her—just thinking about it brought tears to her eyes. She knew then that she had to get help, had to make some changes.

As soon as she was back at her Arizona apartment in January, she had done two things: looked for a therapist, and applied for a new job. Her therapist, Elizabeth, had been a godsend, encouraging a move but cautioning her to take things slowly—the next school year would be better than a sudden change, especially when therapy was going well.

On a whim, Kristina had sent resumes to a private school in Hawaii, an Indian reservation in Wyoming and a special academy for autistic children in Florida. It was a rural school in the mountains of North Carolina, however, that had hired her on the spot for the upcoming school year at the end of her Skype interview.

"We're very excited about the idea of you joining us," the principal had said. "Our special needs class is small, but with someone like you, someone with fresh ideas, I think we can expand." Humphrey K-12 was progressive in mindset if not in finances, she had said. "We can't match your current salary, but you'd make a huge difference here. We sure would like to give you a chance to fall in love with Humphrey."

Not long after graduation, Kristina had been the recipient of a grant. Her first order of business had been to repay her grandparents for their help with tuition, help they could scarcely afford. But whether she'd forgotten ever applying, had lost track of things while she dealt with her trauma, or what, the funds had been tucked away in the bank largely untouched. Until she had found a therapist. And then needed to move. And then needed a new car. Most of the money was still in the bank, though. She decided that she could afford to make less for as long as she needed. She had accepted the position with excitement.

Principal Clark was an attractive black woman with a sweet

smile, gentle manner and infectious laugh. She put Kristina in touch with a realtor, who found several affordable rentals within a ten-mile radius of the school. Her coworkers at home threw her a surprise going away party in July, and now she was finally here. New town, new job. It had taken several days of driving, diners and cheap motels, but she could already anticipate how good it would feel to sleep in her own bed.

It was late afternoon. The sun had already dipped behind the mountains, taking most of the August heat with it. There was still enough light to enjoy her first actual look at the quaint, unpaved street. What she had paid out west for a tiny studio apartment had more than covered the rent on the cute frame, two-bedroom she'd chosen in Poplar Gap.

As soon as she'd gotten confirmation from Principal Clark, she had looked for a place. There were apartments and houses closer to the school, but she'd sent a deposit for this one as soon as she saw the photographs. Circa 1920, it had been updated and refurbished without stealing its original charm. It even had porches—one in the front and one in the back. Two rocking chairs already sat on the front—one for her, one for a friend. *Not that I have any.* But she could already see herself sitting there grading papers or reading a book, waving to the neighbors. Today would be her first step inside.

"Could you use some help?" a cheerful male voice called in a slow drawl, from around the corner of the house. Kristina was pleased that she only jumped inside a *little* bit. "I live behind you, saw your headlights." A man in his sixties, salt and pepper hair framing a smiling milk chocolate face, stepped into the narrow side yard. "Name's Chip. Chip Murphy."

As Chip approached, she caught a strong aroma of hickory smoke. Instinctively, she took a deep breath. The smell had an instant calming effect on her.

"Yeah, I was smokin' a turkey. Just took it out, too. We get this here car unloaded, I'll bring you'uns some dinner."

Without waiting for permission, the man pulled out a box and headed for the front door. "Is it open?"

"Not yet, um, Mr. Murphy. Just set it on the porch. And thank you! I'll be right there." As Kristina followed with another box and the key, she pushed down intruding thoughts connected to every episode of crime TV that involved helpful strangers. This was rural North Carolina, after all. And he was a neighbor, apparently. *Might as well get to know him now. You'uns. As opposed to* y'all? She marveled a little at her frame of mind. A year ago, she wouldn't have spoken to a stranger. *You've come a long way,* she congratulated herself. *Both literally and figuratively.*

Kristina opened the door and flipped on the nearest light switch, drawing in a quick breath. "Isn't it adorable?" The original wood floor of the modest living room was polished to perfection. Bead board walls held a fresh coat of white paint. Someone had even left a vase of fresh flowers on the mantle of the fireplace. For the first time in years, Kristina felt she was home.

"Adorable!" Chip snorted. "It was me who spiffed the place up, and let me tell you, it wasn't adorable till I did! Last renters were real slobs. Didn't deserve anything this nice."

Kristina laughed gaily. "Well, you did a fine job, Mr. Murphy. I love it."

The man muttered loudly all the way back to the car for another load. "Mr. Murphy. I declare. Makes me sound like an old man." Passing her on his way back to the house, he said, "Chip'll do just fine, little lady. And your name is? 'Round these parts, we like to be on whatcha call a 'first name basis'."

Kristina giggled again. Five minutes, and he had already put her fears and misgivings to flight. "I'm Kristina," she called. "Or Kris. Or Tina! Yes! New house, new state—why not a new identity too? I'll be Tina from now on. And you're the first person to know."

Chip was already back for another box, obviously used to hard work. "Well, I'm honored. Tina it is."

"Is Chip short for Charles?" the newly-designated Tina asked, a little out of breath under the weight of a box of dishes.

"Let me get that," he said. "Kitchen, right? No, not Charles, Richard. Boys back in the day called me Cow Chip when I was a young'un, 'cause we had a farm in the sand hills outside Billy Creek. The Chip stuck. Cow didn't." He stood in the kitchen and shook his head with a grin. "I was glad of it, too. Richard sounded too formal, and even as a boy, I didn't want to be called Dick."

Tina winced at the sound of his real name, covering it with a laugh. She'd known a Richard before, and he *had* been a colossal Dick. She was ridiculously pleased to be able to call this man Chip. And what a nice introduction to the community! In much less time than she had anticipated, the car was unloaded while she learned and shared snippets of information as she and Chip passed one another with armloads.

Boxes, suitcases and bags were strewn throughout the house. The owner had agreed to rent the house partially furnished so she didn't have to pull a trailer with furniture, but she could tell she'd need to do some shopping. The bare minimum here would get her started, but… Tina stood in one of the bedrooms and frowned, her hands on her hips.

"Something the matter?" Chip asked as the final bags were deposited inside the bedroom door.

Without a word, Tina pointed to the twin bedstead. The mattress had definitely seen better days.

"Yeah, I pulled that out of storage. Wasn't sure what you'd want. Knew you were a single lady, but…"

Tina patted the man on the arm. "This is fine. Really. I've got a mattress cover and everything. Same size bed back home." *And all the size I'll likely ever need.*

Chip clapped his big hands together, rough from years of hard work. "All righty, then. How about I go fetch us some of that smoked turkey and a couple of cold ones and we sit a spell on the porch?"

By the time Tina waved goodnight to Chip, she felt like she'd gotten a real education. She watched him amble around the corner of her house with his now-empty cooler and a stack of plates, utensils, and assorted condiments. *He's a talker, no doubt about it.* Observant, too, a student of the human race, as he said. She loved the extra syllables to his speech, the cadence that had to mimic what had been heard in these mountains for hundreds of years.

Sitting in the twilight alone, Tina smiled as she remembered their conversation concerning another new tenant. She'd actually live right next door to her. "Maybe we can help move her in," Chip had said. An older woman, he figured she'd need it.

"Too old for me, from the sound of it," he'd continued, shaking his head sadly. "Damn shame, too. Not that many folks like me around these parts." Chip rubbed a hand down one arm for effect. "Not that I make color a stipulation, understand. But here you are, as pretty as a picture and nice as can be, but too young! Now this lady's coming, and she's too old. I need someone right slap in the middle."

Tina had blushed at the compliment, unseen in the dying light of the day. Not so long ago, she would have never sat with a man like that, alone, especially a man she didn't know well. She would have broken out in a cold sweat, trembling, felt trapped, even on an open porch. Her work with Elizabeth had really paid off.

Chip had been raised in the middle of the state, the son of

a struggling farmer and teacher, with many siblings. "It gets hot as blue blazes there. I like the mountains better. We used to come over here on vacation, camp, fish. When I got old enough, I decided to come here permanently. If it wasn't for Mr. Bill, I might not have stayed."

Tina's face flushed again at the memory. She had visibly flinched at the prefix, which sounded to her ears a throwback to darker days. "*Mister* Bill? Does he actually require you to call him that? Doesn't that sound a bit demeaning?"

Chip had thrown his head back and laughed. "Oh, law. You *aren't* from around here. I'll have to remember to tell him. Demeaning. He'd get a kick out of that. We just do things a little different here. *Anyone* older's likely a Mister or Miss, no matter the race. If you know someone, you use their first names, not their last. Young'uns around these parts call me Mr. Chip." He shrugged. "Maybe it's how we tell who belongs and who doesn't. I don't rightly know. But you just call me Chip. I'm not *that* much older than you."

Old enough to be my father, she thought with a sigh. Chip's dog, a beautiful blue pit bull, had joined them at about the third beer, fresh from what was likely an evening of mischief. When she'd asked if he had to have a license, if he worried about Animal Control picking him up, Chip had chuckled again.

"City talk. Everybody here knows Blue, and Blue knows everybody. Fact he isn't growling at *you* is a good thing. I've known him to chase a stranger plumb into the next county."

Tina rocked and closed her eyes, listening to the rush of a breeze through the trees, smelling the mossy air, drinking in the peaceful atmosphere. She looked up and down the little street, a cul-de-sac of sorts. *More like a dead end.* There was a vacant house next door, then another house that Chip said was occupied only during the summer and they'd already packed up. Chip's street was more populated. *Mr. Bill. Good grief.* She wondered how many other local customs she'd get laughed at over. She wasn't going to worry about it. Who could worry about anything with lightning bugs dancing before their eyes?

Finally, she stood up and stretched, luxuriating at the thought of a long, hot shower, but inside, she stopped at the entrance to the bathroom. Involved in unloading the car, she hadn't noticed every detail. The predominant feature of the bathroom was an old claw-foot bathtub. No showerhead. She'd just have to make do for now. Maybe Chip can help. She smiled as she filled the tub with steaming water. *Bubble bath. Put that on the list. And find out if the landlord would mind adding some plumbing. It's either that or cut your hair.*

Even in her most trying times, Tina's hair was her one glory. After… after everything that had happened, she had gone through a rough spot. She stopped wearing make-up and rarely even washed her hair. She'd become a total mess, inside and out. After counseling with Elizabeth, she understood *why* she'd subconsciously tried to cover up her own beauty. She'd worked through that, thankfully.

Her hair, only trimmed since childhood, hung below her waist. She usually wore it up, tight braids wrapped around her head like a crown or in one long braid down her back. She liked the versatility that long, straight hair afforded, but a shower would definitely make maintenance easier. Tonight, she'd make do with the tub, eager to make up the bed and finally get some rest.

Just as she took off her clothes and was about to step into the deep pool of water, her cell phone rang from the bedroom. Quickly, she pulled a towel from the hamper she'd packed linens in and wrapped it around herself—no curtains up yet. *Maybe I'll use the other room for storage, maybe an office.* "Hello?"

From hundreds of miles away, Layla sighed with relief. "I was getting worried. You *always* call by now to let me know you're okay." A single woman driving cross-country needed to keep communication lines open, she'd cautioned her sister.

"I'm sorry, Lay. I totally forgot with everything. I made it here about, oh, five o'clock, then Chip and I unloaded, and he brought me dinner, and—"

"Chip?"

Tina laughed. "Leave it to you to focus on that. Yes, I met a man. A neighbor, and no, I'm not falling in love with him and getting married." There was nothing to do but provide an in-depth description of her final day on the road and the colorful Mr. Murphy, so Tina walked back into the little bathroom, dropped the towel, and continued the conversation from the tub.

"This Tina business will take some getting used to," Layla said as the sisters said goodnight.

"Feel free to call me Kristina or Kris, whatever you want." Tina giggled. "I just thought it was the perfect time to start fresh."

After she laid the phone on the floor, Tina sank down further into the tub until she was submerged. *Ahhh*. She had wanted a shower, but a long, hot bath had its own glories. She came up for air and leaned her head back against the end of the tub, swirling the water slowly with her hands, running them along her body, up and down her bent legs. She was too tired to shave her legs tonight. *Why bother anyway? No one would notice.*

One hand hesitated. She let it wander where it wanted to go, between her legs. *Find the little button*, she thought. *Make me feel alive. Make me feel like a woman.*

She experienced no sensation. It wasn't that touching the area was unpleasant. It was no different than touching her leg or arm. It should be different. *Elizabeth said it would take time for the remnants of trauma to heal. I've got plenty of that, anyway.*

Chip Murphy rocked on his back porch until he saw the last light go out in Tina's house. If Tina didn't hang curtains the next day, he'd be surprised. She'd walked into that back bedroom with nothing on but a towel, quickly switching the light off. Feeling suddenly proprietary, he decided that if she hadn't hung curtains by noon tomorrow, he'd walk over and see if she needed help. Friendly's one thing, but she needed privacy. A quiet place to just be, away from prying eyes. Mr. Bill had taught him that.

"She sure is purty, isn't she, old boy?" he asked Blue softly, scratching him between the ears then heading for his screen door. "Mr. Bill asked us to be on the look-out for one, and she might do just fine. We'll have to see, won't we? Come on then. Our job's done for the day."

2

Girls' Night In

"I'm telling you, it did my heart good," Layla told the other ladies who were sitting comfortably in the living room. Her husband Keith, a teacher, had a meeting at school, providing the perfect time for a girls' night. "Kris sounded like herself for sure. Or should we all start calling her Tina? Apparently, that's how she introduced herself in North Carolina."

Layla's sister-in-law Kari brought in a bottle of wine from the kitchen and refilled any glasses that needed it. "I think we should switch, too. Tina's simpler, and it kind of signifies that we recognize she's a new person these days. What do you think, Carol?"

Carol Henderson was both girls' stepmother now, having married Kari's father—Layla's father-in-law—not quite a year earlier. Carol had known the Henderson kids through their parents for many years before their mother passed away from cancer and her own husband died in a fire. Chet Henderson had been his boss at the fire department.

Carol's hair was a little grayer than when she'd been a bride, but she had the happy confidence of a woman who is loved and appreciated by her man. She'd been a nurse, a homemaker, a nurse again, and now the wife of a retired fire chief and mom to an extended family. Carol was in her element, pleased that the younger ladies of the family made it a point to include her and, on occasion, ask her opinion and advice.

"I agree with Kari," she said, sipping her Shiraz. "From what you've told me, she's gone through an amazing metamorphosis. Calling her Tina acknowledges that we notice and reinforces our support."

Just then the plump infant on the blanket on the floor let out a cry. Unnoticed, Angela had turned over while the ladies chatted. She didn't appear to be scared, just surprised that she was no longer looking at a pastel plaid blanket, but into five delighted faces.

Jessica, Carol's daughter, was the first to scoop the baby up, holding her over her head and cooing, "What a smart little girl you are! Turning over when we're all here to congratulate you." Jessica had been waiting to share her own big news. This seemed as good a time as any. "And speaking of congratulations…" Handing Angela to her best friend Donna, Jessica patted her stomach dramatically.

Carol sprung off the couch to hug her daughter. "I *wondered* why you hadn't touched your wine. I am so happy for you and Worth! When are you due? Do you know if it's a boy or a girl? Have you picked out names?"

Jessica laughed and sat back down. "In the spring, no, and no. I just found out this week."

Donna, Jessica's friend and coworker, shook her head, beaming, taking Angela's little fists in her hands to wiggle them back and forth. "I'll bet Worth is over the moon. Molly, too." Worth's mother owned the magazine they both wrote for, insisting that everyone address her as Molly, even her son, editor Worth Vincent.

Jessica giggled. "Unless we can stop her, I think she's planning to send an interior decorator over from Paris to do the nursery."

The women continued to chat for a few minutes until Angela started crying. "Dinner time," Layla announced as Donna handed her over. "Mind if I feed her here?"

A chorus of "noes" and "of course nots" made her smile. She reached under her blouse to unsnap her nursing bra and guided her nipple into Angela's hungry mouth. Soon the room was filled with soft slurps and swallows as Layla's milk let down and Angela took her fill of first one breast, then the other. The other women chatted and laughed.

Carol sighed. "I did miss that, once Jessica was weaned. We thought we'd have more children, but—"

"I guess it just wasn't meant to be," her daughter said. "Worth and I aren't going to make definite plans, either. 'See what happens, see how many." She made a face. "Easy for me to say *now*! I may change my tune after the third or fourth!"

"Or eighth or ninth!" Kari laughed. "But seriously, Layla, I'm so glad Kristina, um, *Tina*, is doing well. Can you tell us more? I mean, what *happened* that turned everything around. And… well, I don't want you to betray any confidences, but what went wrong in the first place?"

Layla looked down at the nursing Angela, stroking her cheek. "You know, growing up in southern California, we always missed having a mother. We were so young when they had the accident." She looked around the room with tears in her eyes. "We were blessed to have grandparents who could raise us, truly blessed, but now that I'm a mother, I just… I can't imagine what it would be like to know your daughter had been…"

It was her senior year at an elite college in Arizona, just over the California border. Kristina Edwards divided her time between interning at local Exceptional Student Education classes and finishing her course requirements. Some of the kids she worked with just broke her heart. Several students had obvious disabilities, such as deafness or blindness. Others had been born with Down Syndrome or spina bifida. They all tried so hard, though, and had amazing attitudes.

Others were "differently abled" as one of her teachers called it—intellectually or emotionally impaired, brain injured, or on the autism spectrum. Outwardly, they looked like any other child, but inwardly, they struggled. Kristina found herself gravitating to the autistic students, a few of whom could not communicate verbally or show affection. She told her advisor that she planned to work with autistic kids exclusively at some point.

It was finally Friday. After a tough day of interning, she was ready to relax. Usually, she spent time reading and listening to music in her dorm room—she earned a little extra cash as the Resident Assistant on the hall—but today, on her way to the dorm, she was stopped outside the student union by a class-mate, a guy she'd never spoken to beyond the occasional "Hey."

"Kristina, right?" He was said to be from a wealthy family, played golf for the college, and was the best looking guy on campus, in her opinion. She couldn't believe he was talking to her.

"Yes," she said shyly. "And you're… Richard?"

"Richard Barrows, at your service." He grinned with a little flourish of his hand. "Listen, some buddies of mine are playing a gig at one of the frat houses, pretty good jazz. Would you like to go with?"

"Go with?"

"With me, on a date." He frowned. "I mean, unless you've

already got plans. It's kind of late notice. A pretty girl like you probably already has a date. I should have thought of that." He held up his hands in defeat. "I apologize."

What a sweet thing to say. "As it so happens, I do *not* have plans tonight," Kristina murmured. "It's been a rough week—a night out would be nice. What time should I be ready? Or do you want me to meet you there?"

Richard smiled and nodded. "*That* would be great. I offered to go early and help them set up, so if you meet me, you wouldn't have to tag along and just be sitting. They don't start playing until nine." He pulled out a little paper from his shirt pocket, scribbling directions and his cell number down in case she needed it. "I've got class, but see you tonight!"

Kristina took the paper and tucked it into a side pocket of her backpack. *I have a date! He's not picking me up at the door and driving me to dinner, but it's a bona fide date.*

Not her first date, of course. She'd had crushes in high school, a few brief and unsatisfying encounters at college. She was so intent on her education, she'd never had anything remotely resembling a steady boyfriend. Her grandparents had sacrificed for Layla and her to go to college, and she yearned to make them proud. There would be plenty of time for guys later. Hadn't she just introduced her sister to one of the teachers at the school where she interned? Layla had crossed the border for lunch with Kristina, and she had "just happened" to seat them close to Keith.

Layla had been the more popular sister in high school, but now it looked like she had found "the one." Keith Henderson was tall, boyishly good-looking, a middle school social studies teacher. Raised back east, he'd taken his current job to expand his horizons, launch out on his own. One look at Layla, and Kristina could tell they were made for each other.

Perhaps I'm made for Richard Barrows, she thought with a giggle. *Stranger things have happened.*

Kristina was grateful that RAs got rooms to themselves. She wouldn't have wanted a roommate observing her uncharacteristically frantic search for the perfect outfit. Everything she owned was either bought on sale or something Layla had grown tired of. *Too stuffy. Too tight. Too low-cut.* She didn't want to give the wrong idea. She gazed at her reflection in the mirror. *Well, maybe a* little *of the wrong idea. Oh, don't be stupid.*

Finally, when there was a pile of discarded choices heaped on the bed, she contented herself with a pale green-and-navy sundress with a navy shrug and navy flats. It had pockets, so she could put her keys and ID there and not have to bother with a purse. Money? Probably no need at a frat party. Not that she'd ever been to one.

Kristina carefully applied her makeup at the little sink in the corner of her room. Mascara, a little liner, foundation, blush. Long-lasting lipstick, the label said. *Maybe I'll actually need that tonight.* Hair. The braids kept things neat, but a frat party wasn't the place for that regal crown, something Layla frequently teased her about, calling it her Amish look.

Kristina sat on the edge of her bed, taking out a dozen hairpins and the elastic bands. She carefully unbraided her hair and combed it with her fingers. *Too bushy to wear down.* She pulled it back in a single hair tie, re-braided it and added a green ribbon at the top for flourish. One last look at the mirror at 8:45 revealed a stylish, pretty young woman who had spent time getting ready but hadn't gone overboard. *You'll do.*

Campus police were always visible, and the campus was well lit; Kristina wasn't concerned about walking a few blocks by herself at night. The fraternity and sorority houses were on a single stretch of street about a half-mile from her dorm, populated with wealthier and more popular students. The particular house she was headed to was one of the oldest on campus, a monstrosity in gray slate, with red doors and shutters.

As she walked up the sidewalk, she saw that the front door was open. From what she could hear already, Richard's assessment of the "pretty good jazz" had been modest. *This is going to be great.*

Suddenly, all of Kristina's inherent shyness reared its head. Why had he asked *her*, when he could get a date with anyone on campus? She was an RA, so not wealthy. She was confident of her studies, but socially, she preferred Layla's company to a throng of college friends. *He's probably got other girls here, intends to pawn me off on another guy. When I step inside, he'll be surrounded by beautiful girls in skimpy dresses and high heels.*

As she stepped into the frat house, however, Richard broke away from a clump of guys and greeted her with a brief but genuine hug. "I'm so glad you made it all right!" he murmured in her ear. "I hated not picking you up properly, but I'd told them I'd help before I got up the nerve to ask you." He stepped back a little with a wave of his hand toward the band.

Is this guy for real? "Your friends are really talented," she said loudly, so that he could hear her over the music.

Richard nodded, guiding her by the elbow to where several short sofas and chairs were arranged. "Can I get you a drink?"

"Sure! Thanks. Whatever you're having."

Richard wrinkled his nose. "I'm a Scotch man. Unless you're used to it, it can kick your butt. How about wine?"

Kristina's face flushed. *I guess I don't look the part for Scotch. That was considerate of him.*

Richard and Kristina sat on the sofa listening to the music, sipping their drinks. There were probably fifty other students there, with more expected later. "Do you live here?" she asked.

He gave her a curious look. "Um, no. Did you want to see—"

She blushed. "Oh, no! I just wondered."

Richard chuckled and took one of Kristina's hands. "It's

okay! I was just surprised. You seem like such a nice girl, I wasn't expecting the question."

Kristina nodded. "I *am* a nice girl, Richard. A nice girl who's worked hard all week. This is a great way to spend my Friday night. Good music, good wine—"

Richard took the empty glass from her and stood. "Time for a refill. Hey, here's Todd. Talk to my date while I'm gone?"

Todd, she knew, was also on the golf team, also from money. Blond and tan, he'd never spoken to her before, but she was grateful to have company in the room of virtual strangers while Richard got her wine. Todd handed her a bowl of pretzels from a nearby table as he sat down in a chair across from her. "Want some?" As she reached for a handful, he chatted in a smooth, deep voice. "Todd Bailey." He rolled his eyes a little and added, "Junior."

"Kristina."

"Your first time?"

"First—"

"Time. At the frat house. Hearing this band. Dating Richard."

"All of the above. The band's really good," Kristina said, hoping there wasn't pretzel residue between her teeth. *Jeez. I've been studying so hard, I hadn't noticed how handsome so many of the guys around here are.*

Richard handed her a bigger glass of wine as he winked at Todd and sat back down beside Kristina. Todd flashed a grin. "Have you introduced Kristina to Mitch yet?" Without waiting for an answer, he waved a big, strapping redhead over from across the room.

"Hey, guys! Who's this beautiful lady?" He reached out a hand, which Kristina shook briefly. There was just enough room for him to sit down on the small sofa on the other side of her. "Beautiful lady sandwich!" he said, laughing a little too loudly at his own joke.

Kristina could smell the liquor on his breath. She leaned forward a little to sip her wine.

"Kristina Edwards, Mitch O'Day," Richard introduced. "Also a jock, a golfer and a bit of an asshole."

Mitch snorted. "Watch your mouth, Barrows. Virgin ears present."

"Not for long," Todd said almost too softly for her to hear.

Is it that *obvious I'm a virgin? We're here not for long? Maybe there's an after party somewhere else.* Her thoughts were getting a bit muddled. Kristina sipped more of the delicious wine. She'd never had more than one glass or one beer before, and she could tell it was getting to her. *Dancing would be fun.* "Will there be danshing? Dancing. Dan. Sing." Her tongue felt funny, too thick for her mouth.

Richard put an arm around her shoulders. "There will indeed be *danshing.*" He and the other guys laughed. "Why don't we make our way onto the floor right about now... finish your wine like a good little girl, and we'll go trip the light fantastic."

Kristina turned the wine glass up to catch the last few drops then stood up on wobbly knees. As she started to sit back down, Richard effortlessly grabbed her up in his arms. "There you go. Unsteady? That's okay. We've got plenty of room on the floor. I'll carry you like this. It'll be fun!"

He was right. Richard twirled her around and around on the dance floor as the bass guitar thumped the beat. When she closed her eyes, she felt like she was dancing across the piano keys, making music. The drum sped up. Richard was twirling her faster and faster and—

Richard looked down at Kristina and kissed her passionately, more passionately than she could remember ever being kissed, kissed, mist. Missed. She missed her sister, missed her parents, she tried to say and then dozed off in Richard's arms. Richard signaled Mitch and Todd with a nod. No one was paying attention to one more couple necking on the dance floor. No one noticed as Richard carried her up the staircase. No one noticed the two others follow.

Blinding sunlight woke Kristina the next morning. Her head felt as though it would split in two. She was alone in a lounge chair. Kristina looked frantically around and saw that she was in the walled yard behind the fraternity house. Everything hurt. *Probably from sleeping outside in the damp night air.*

When she stood up, there was blood on the cushion.

Carol Henderson wiped a tear from her cheek. "That poor girl," she whispered. "She never told you who it was?"

"I don't think *she* even knew," Layla said sadly, rocking the now sleeping Angela in her arms. "The boy she'd met there said she had too much to drink, was dancing with everyone there. He was so disgusted, he left the party early with two of his friends. They corroborated his story. So as far as she knows, she either had sex with someone she met there, or she was raped after she passed out drunk. She wasn't… forthcoming with all the details. Either way, she was so ashamed of losing her virginity in a drunken stupor that it *really* did a number on her."

Donna's eyes were narrow and hard. "Someone like her, who's never had even the *hint* of a mark against her? My vote's on rape. I'd like to get my hands on whoever is responsible." *And my whip.* Donna and her husband Eric enjoyed some rather interesting adult toys that they used for lovemaking. But the toys could have darker uses, too.

Kari shook her head slowly, as if she still couldn't believe it. It all made sense now. Kristina's depression, her disheveled appearance. A paralegal, she'd heard of cases like this following a rape. "Some women want to stop being feminine.

Like being pretty was the problem. As if they invited the rape because they dressed a certain way." She sighed. "I wish there was something we could do, but it sounds like she's gotten it figured out in the meantime."

Layla put Angela up on one shoulder to burp her in her sleep. Patting the baby softly on the back, she lowered her voice. "Lots of therapy, with a woman who really knows her stuff. Elizabeth something."

Jessica had listened to Layla's account in stunned silence. "I'm confused, though. The timeline. She went to the party and woke up alone, and then what?"

"She had the presence of mind to go to the campus infirmary, where the nurse had *some* SANE training—for Sexual Abuse Nurse Examiner. Kristina had definitely had sex, *rough* sex, a lot of it. There was… bruising. But there was no semen. Whoever it was, was careful. She also didn't think that it had happened on the lounge chair. Not enough blood. The nurse wanted to call the cops, but Kristina refused. She couldn't prove anything. This was before she got wind of Richard's story, too. She couldn't imagine why he would have left her there, why he didn't call her. She called *him* instead."

"What did he say?"

Layla's face was grim. "He didn't take the call."

"But who did the guys tell their side of things to?"

Angela whimpered a bit in her sleep, so Layla stood and swayed back and forth to soothe her. "They told the golf team coach they were concerned their names might come up in an investigation, so they took the initiative and explained the situation. The coach stopped by her internship to check on her—that was nice, right? Just wait till you hear. He told her what Richard, Todd, and Mitch had said. 'You need to be more careful,' he told her. 'Is that how you were raised?'"

Jessica was furious. "Nice? I think not! He *assumed* it was her fault. That's *terrible*! Those golfers had something to do with it. Put something in her drink. Made up the whole thing."

Layla stopped swaying, her face pale. "I-I hadn't thought of that. She was *so* sure it was her fault. She's convinced that she got drunk and made a fool out of herself. When she managed to catch up to Richard a few days later, he said he didn't think it would work out after the frat party debacle. 'Debacle.' He actually said 'debacle'! He said she had embarrassed him. She was *mortified*. She started feeling as though people were looking at her differently, talking about her. She graduated, but only just. Her grades went down, she was written up a few times at the dorm and at her school. She took a nosedive all around."

Carol sat back against the couch. Kristina's story had drained her. She'd met her the Christmas before and had been very taken by her quiet helpfulness, but also touched by the sadness in her eyes. Now she understood. "I'm with you, Jessica," she said with restrained anger. "I'd bet money that those three Neanderthals were involved. Three little rich boys whose daddies would never let them see the inside of a jail, even if they *were* caught."

Layla caught Donna's eye. "Would you put her down, Donna? Rich boys. You know, Kristina was awarded a scholarship a few months after graduation, a grant, really, for autism specialists just starting out," she said, pausing for impact. "She hadn't *applied* for a grant. And no one she asked was familiar with the foundation that issued it."

"*That* smells fishy," Kari said wryly. "How much was the grant?"

"Three hundred thousand dollars."

Kari whistled. "Interesting amount. *Three*. Hundred thousand. Not one. Not two, but three. That's some grant!"

Jessica nodded. "Honestly, I'd wondered where she came up with the money to relocate and buy that brand new SUV, but I wasn't going to ask. Therapy's expensive, too."

As Donna returned from the nursery, Jessica leaned in, pulling her mother and friends into a tighter circle. "If you remember, Worth was on the run practically his whole life, accused of that fatal fire as a child. His mother staged his suicide so they could start over somewhere else, right? Along the way, he and Molly developed quite a network of resources. Would you mind if I told him Kristina's story? *Tina's* story? See if he'd be willing to look into it? There might be nothing there, but—"

Tears streamed freely down Layla's face. "Mind? *Anything* that would help her find peace. She's come a long way already, but to find out what really happened? I can't see how that could be anything but beneficial. *Thank* you."

3

School Begins

As Tina slowed the SUV for yet another hairpin curve in the road linking her house to her new job, she thought back on the first week of school. There had been a week of preparation, accompanied by many meetings, many forms to fill out.

On Monday, Tina had somewhat timidly pointed out that the walls of the ESE room were badly in need of painting, only to be told that there were no funds left in the budget. During the lunch break, Tina drove to Humphrey Hardware and bought five gallons of deep green paint, a color that sometimes had a calming effect on autistic children.

She and the other ESE teacher and aide painted into the early evening. When it was dry, bulletin boards were festooned with trim and important reminders. Laminated nametags were affixed to every desk. Tina felt that she would get along well with the rest of her team and the faculty and staff as a whole. She was especially fond of Principal Clark.

Tina smiled. She felt strong again. Independent. She'd mistaken a focus on her studies for a lack of emotional neediness, but the Richard business had proved otherwise. She'd been devastated. Elizabeth had been extremely helpful, although therapy had not been easy. Tina truly believed that she had no need for a man in her life, not romantically at any rate. That particular door, open for however long the unfortunate events at the frat party had taken, had closed forever.

It wasn't that she felt unworthy, although she had to admit that a few stubborn traces of shame lingered. She was back to taking care of her health and her appearance, but it was for *herself* that she primped now.

Already, the weather was cooling down, unseasonably so. She opened all the windows as she drove, breathing in the unique, ancient smell of the mountains. So much had changed in the last few months. She'd made life-changing headway with Elizabeth, driven cross-country, met Chip. She thought about getting her hair cut, a monumental decision. *Mmm. Not just yet.*

Thinking of hair and maintenance turned her thoughts downward. Layla had asked her about getting a bikini wax, something she'd never considered. Keith wasn't wild about the idea, but what did Tina think? *Tina doesn't really care about lady-scaping,* she thought as the wind blew across her face. *It's not like anyone besides my doctor will ever see* my *bush.*

As she pulled into her gravel driveway, she spotted Chip doing yard work next door, in preparation for the new tenant. When she waved, he held out his clippers. "Want me to trim your bush?"

Tina threw back her head and laughed, confusing Chip completely. "I'm sorry. You caught me off guard," she said, choking a little. *No way am I explaining* that *one.* "The planter looks nice. When is the old lady coming?" The old lady. That was the way they always talked about her.

Chip walked over to open the car door for her as Tina gathered her lunch bag and papers. "Any day. She doesn't drive, Mr. Bill says, so she's waiting for somebody to bring her and her things. Likely more 'things' than you had when you got here. Women," he muttered with a grin. "'Longer they live, the more stuff they accumulate."

Tina nodded, glancing at the gardenia bush by her mailbox. It was indeed getting rangy. "I see what you mean," she said, pointing. "If you want to trim it, that'd be great."

Walking into the house, she chuckled, mentally replaying the last few minutes so that she could tell Layla word for word.

"Yes, Mr. Bill, it's all ready for the old lady. House is spic and span, yard's tidy. I put new flowers in the planter today and did some trimming for Tina, too. She sure is nice." Chip held the phone with one hand as he unlaced his boots with the other. Blue curled up at his feet for a nap on the braided rug.

The soft laugh on the other end spoke of years of shared amusement. "I'll thank you not to call anyone my age 'old', Chip," Bill Cameron said. He had walked up the mountain to the cell tower to check on things, a formality. Since he'd given permission to the company to erect it, there had been very few mishaps. Bad weather might interfere, but he was pleased to provide the community with reliable service. Only a handful of people realized his part in things, but that was the way he wanted it. "Tell me more about this Tina," he continued. "Do you think she and Ian would hit it off?"

Chip frowned. The whole plan seemed sketchy to him, and he'd said so on more than one occasion. But Mr. Bill was the boss, so whatever he wanted, Chip would go along with. He hadn't had a great deal of experience with romantic meetings, but this one seemed fraught with risk. She might not like him. He might not like her. She might be mad at *him*, which he certainly did not want. A planned, but seemingly unplanned, meeting could go either way. Love at first sight, or bitter hate.

"I think Ian's a great guy, a fine man. You raised him well.

And from what I can tell so far, Tina is the finest young woman I've *ever* met. On the surface, you know, that might mean they'd hit it off. It's *under* the surface that concerns me."

Chip kicked off his boots and settled back into his favorite armchair. Pretty soon, it would be cool enough for a fire of an evening. Late August, early September, it could be hot still, but this year, all the signs pointed to a fierce and early winter. He read the *Farmer's Almanac* with almost as much fervor as he read the Bible and the weekly newspaper. There had been heavier fog this month, and danged if he hadn't seen woodpeckers doubling up on some trees.

Even Mr. Bill had pointed out a hornet's nest in a poplar tree the last time they'd hiked together. Clucking his tongue, he'd pointed it out. "Hard winter this year, I wager. My daddy always said, 'See how high the hornet's nest, 'twill tell how high the snow will rest.' I've never seen a nest that big, nor that high up in the branches."

Now, Bill Cameron made a nondescript noise in his throat. "You know I may not have much longer, Chip. I need him to find a woman before I go, and the pickings have been mighty slim. Most folks move to the big cities, although I've yet to hear a good reason."

Chip said nothing. He couldn't love this man more if he was his own father. He knew the man had endured more than most. His first love had been packed off and sent away by her parents to keep them apart. He'd married a fine woman who had given him a son before she died of pneumonia. He'd raised the boy on the mountain and later welcomed his wife, a Cherokee. When she died in childbirth, though, his son couldn't take the pain. He'd drunk himself to death one winter, dying of exposure. Ian, Bill's grandson, was his whole world, that and his mountain. Chip guessed he could understand the urgency, but he couldn't bear the thought of losing his closest and oldest friend.

"How're you feeling?" he asked.

"Oh, you know. Fair to middlin'. Getting by. More tired than usual. Sorer."

Safely distanced in his living room, Chip rolled his eyes and shook his head. Blue raised his head sleepily as if in agreement. "Dagnabbit, Mr. Bill, you're eighty! Everybody's tired and sore at eighty."

Bill Cameron chuckled. "So you say, so you say. And maybe you're right. But my daddy died before he was eighty, and his daddy before him, as far back as the family Bible's records go, and that's all the way back to the 1700s. No man in my family has lasted longer than I have already. I can feel it. Just a matter of time, and I can't leave without doing right by Ian. Not if I can help it."

A few weeks later, the "old lady" was yet to arrive. "I wonder what the delay is?" Tina asked Chip as she stirred her mashed potatoes. The friends were enjoying a rare night out at Francine's Diner, the only eating establishment for ten miles, and the best (in their opinion) for twenty-five.

Tina had been offended by the prominent Confederate flag outside on the porch, but Chip was characteristically dismissive, not a man to pay much attention to such things. "Good eats ain't about politics. Francine's got good eats."

"You want some mashed 'taters with that butter?" he teased now.

"I like butter," she said, defiantly putting a huge forkful into her mouth.

Chip signaled to Francine for a refill of his sweet tea. "I got a call from Mr. Bill today, and he says to look for her tomorrow. Course we've heard that before, but maybe this time it's a fact."

Tina made a face and wiped her mouth. "Darn it. I wanted

to help her move in, but I was hoping to go explore the mountain."

Chip put down his fork, suddenly serious. "Don't you go hiking around *Cameron* Mountain, you hear? It's got electric fencing for a reason. Lotta bears on Cameron Mountain. You stay away, now." He relaxed a little. "You want to go exploring, wait for me. I can take you to some waterfalls, the best fishing spots, anything you want."

"I suppose I could help her tomorrow and explore on Sunday. You said it was going to be a cold winter, though. Early one. I want to look around while I can."

"Young'uns, always in a hurry." Chip took the tea from Francine with a lecherous wink. As soon as the ample-busted owner had walked back behind the counter, he whispered, "That woman can cook up a lot more than country style steak, if you get my drift."

Tina blushed. "Chip Murphy, as I live and breathe," she cooed. "Are you sweet on Miss Francine?"

"A gentleman doesn't talk about such things," he sniffed, buttering a small, hot biscuit. Copious amounts of fresh blackberry jam followed the butter. When the biscuit was suitably prepared, Chip popped it into his mouth.

"Would you like a little biscuit with your jam?" Tina asked dryly. "But seriously, you and Francine?" Holding both hands above her plate, she entwined the fingers as she wiggled her eyebrows suggestively.

Chip grinned. "Let's just say that Miss Francine may be the great-great-great-great-granddaughter of a Confederate war hero, but she's color blind under the sheets."

Tina shook her head in amusement. "Mr. Murphy, you constantly surprise me. I'm glad you've got someone."

Her genial friend crossed his arms and stared at her for a moment. "Having someone once in a while isn't the same as *having* someone. I'm still looking for the woman who can put up with me 24/7. I 'spect I'll have to venture away from here to find such an oddity, but you never know. Sure wish you were a little older."

Tina reached over and laid a hand gently on Chip's arm. "Thank you. Really. That means a lot. I never knew my father, but I guess he'd be about your age now. I think he'd be as impressed with you as I am. You've been nothing but helpful and kind to me." She resumed eating. "Are you this nice to all Mr. Bill's tenants?"

The mention of the man brought back memories of their last conversation. The sudden realization that this time next year, Mr. Bill might be gone brought tears to Chip's eyes.

"What's the matter? What did I say wrong?" Tina was horrified that she might have hurt his feelings.

Chip blew his nose on his brown paper napkin. "You said nary a word wrong. I just remembered something that made me sad." He looked at Tina and smiled. "Everybody leaves, that's all. I've never really gotten used to it."

"Who's left, Chip? I mean, if you don't mind talking about it?"

As Chip told his story, the two of them finished their meal, paid the bill and walked out into the cool evening. When Tina shivered against the chill air, he gallantly laid his thick flannel jacket across her shoulders as he talked.

He was adopted, he said, so his parents had been the first to leave him. He never heard the details, probably never would. He'd been given to an agency at the state capital for placement, staying in several foster homes as an infant until the Murphys adopted him. Billy Creek is about an hour from Raleigh, a bit closer to Fayetteville, he told her, out in the middle of farmland, not much of a town at all. He'd ridden the bus to school in the next town over, had graduated from the only high school in the county.

"Small town, good people. Church every Sunday and

Wednesday night, prayer meeting on Saturday night. Daddy was a farmer, and pretty good at it, although no farmer has it easy, even if you aren't just about the only black farmer in the county. Raised goats, mostly, meat and milk. Mama was a schoolteacher, getting along in years. They'd wanted a big family but no luck. She quit teaching, though," he said with a chuckle, "'cause after they adopted me, the dam burst. She popped a young'un out every year for the next five and then stopped. Six of us to feed, and we all turned out as nice as me."

Tina was intrigued. "They're still in the middle part of the state? How often do you get to see them?"

By this time, they were walking down the road to Tina's house. The moon was high above them, but too small in the sky to cast much light on the path. "Maybe once a year, at Thanksgiving or Christmas. We're maybe five, six hours from there, but we all stay so busy. Mama and Daddy passed away, first Mama, then Daddy a few months later. Don't know if we'll have a reunion this year—what with the early winter, and a bad one to boot. I may need to stick around to help Mr. Bill with everything."

Tina kept her unkind thoughts about the elusive Mr. Bill to herself. Chip thought highly of him, but he had not even gone to the trouble of meeting his tenant. True, he'd been amenable to the addition of the showerhead and had paid for everything, but it just seemed odd in such a friendly community for someone to be such a hermit. No one she'd questioned had much to say about Bill Cameron, other than to say he was rarely seen and that his family had been some of the area's first settlers.

"Maybe Mr. Bill will want to meet the old lady, anyway," she sniffed. "If I'm around, I'd like to finally meet him, too."

Chip took his jacket back as she stepped onto her porch. "I 'spect you'll meet Mr. Bill real soon, Tina. *Real* soon. Don't you worry about that."

Far be it from me to worry about a man of any *age*, she thought. "Whatever you say. Want to have a cold one before you go?" After spending so much time alone, she was finding it less and less enjoyable, now that she'd met Chip. He was so easy to talk to. Maybe the age difference made her more comfortable. He was complimentary and flirtatious at times, but she knew it was all an act. His attitude was more paternal than anything. She felt safe with him. Safer than she had felt in a long time.

Chip was thinking that Mr. Bill had managed to insinuate himself into a perfectly nice conversation without even being there. His outrageous plan to acquire a woman for his grandson, as it grew closer by the day, inspired caution. Maybe he should back off a little from this delightful young woman. Soon, she might *hate* him as much as she seemed now to adore him. *You just never know with women folks.* "No, that's okay," he said, suddenly gruff. "I'm turning in early, in case the old lady shows up. Heap of work if she does. But thank you."

Tina hid her disappointment. She did have papers to grade and student assessments to complete. She'd call Layla, maybe turn in early herself. "If I don't wake up in time to help, bang on the door, okay? 'Night."

4

Worth Has a Thought

"What in the wide world of sports is that?" Worth was stretched out on the bed making a few notes on a pad for the next day at the magazine, but a splash of color caught his eye. Jessica was leaning against the doorway in a turquoise negligee.

Jessica turned so that her back rested against the frame and pulled a generous amount of the filmy fabric away from her body. She giggled. "Layla gave me this maternity nightgown when we had our girls' night. There's definitely room to grow."

Worth snorted. "You aren't even showing yet. And I expect I'll enjoy your naked *pregnant* body as much as ever. Therefore," he said as he leapt off the bed and picked her up in his arms, "the nightgown is strictly *verboten*." He dropped her unceremoniously on the bed and leaned over her for a kiss.

"Hmm," she murmured. "Maybe I like wearing turquoise tents."

Worth laughed as he stood. His robe fell open as he did, and Jessica raised her eyebrows. "Why, Mr. Vincent," she said. "You seem to be a bit excited. Maybe deep down, you've needed me to cover up more. Layla's nightgown appears to have turned you on.""

"Deep is where I'm heading, my dear," Worth whispered, "as soon as you take that monstrosity off." The robe dropped to the floor. Jessica reached up to tickle Worth's rippled abdomen, tracing a line from his navel to his cock, which she pulled gently, drawing him down.

Giggling, Jessica wriggled her way out of the yards of material. "My stomach is still flat, but I think my breasts are getting bigger. Could you take a closer look and see?"

Worth laid her back on the bed and began kissing them, licking her nipples, taking one in his mouth while his fingers pulled gently at the other. His free hand stroked her side, her hip and then her soft triangle of hair. Jessica moaned as his fingers moved between her legs. Gently, he thrust two fingers inside.

Jessica rocked her hips, meeting his pressure as waves of pleasure swept over her. Fiercely, she grabbed his torso, pulling him away from her breasts, pulling his hand from between her legs.

Worth got up on his hands and knees and gazed down at her. He'd always heard that pregnancy gave women a special glow, but he'd never paid attention. It was true. Jessica had never looked more beautiful to him than she did at that moment, her brown hair spread across the pillow, her eyes looking up at him with desire.

Jessica reached again for his erection, lubricating the tip with a drop of his own moisture, kneading him with a strong grip until his eyes closed in the intensity of sensation. She shifted her position slightly and guided him inside. "I want you inside me, love," she commanded.

So aroused were both of them, that they reached their climax together only moments later. Worth rolled Jessica to her side and they lay, still joined, as their breath began to slow.

Jessica's leg circled his hip as his hand cupped a breast. Jessica lifted her chin for a kiss as Worth grew inside of her again.

"How do you do that?" she murmured appreciatively.

"Love, everything about you turns me on. Except for the nightgown," he said with a chuckle. He began rocking his hips slowly.

"Hmm?"

"Don't mind me," he whispered. "You go on to sleep. I'm going to play a bit longer."

Jessica rolled on top of him. "Oh, no, you don't. You play, I play." Lovemaking wasn't the only thing that made their relationship incredible, but it was an important part of it. "Will it always be like this for us?" she asked as she straightened her elbows and gave him a better view as they moved together gently.

Worth pulled her firmly by her buttocks. "Always." She leaned down to kiss him as their movements quickened. Jessica gave a little cry of delight as she climaxed and began to slow down, but Worth would have none of it. Bucking harder and harder, his face contorted in concentration as he exploded inside of her.

This time when he rolled her onto her side, he withdrew from her and sprawled on his back, his eyes closed. Curled against him, she played with the dense hair on his chest. "Are all the men on your planet this skillful at pleasuring Earth women?"

Worth didn't open his eyes but nodded with a smile. After a few minutes, he leaned over to gently kiss her on the mouth. "We are so blessed, aren't we? Turn over; I want to kiss your neck."

He turned off the bedside lamp as she complied and pulled the covers up over them. Nestled together, Jessica took his free hand and cupped it around her breast. Worth kissed her neck sweetly. "Goodnight, love."

"Goodnight."

Jessica was completely relaxed. She kept meaning to talk to Worth about Kristina—Tina—but it would wait until morning.

"Hey, Jess?" Worth whispered.

"Mmm?"

"I think your breasts *are* bigger."

Worth's assistant Skip handed him the trip itinerary to approve and left. Worth had listened with growing concern as Jessica shared with him what she knew of Kristina Edwards' trouble at college. He agreed that the story her frat party date had spun was just that: a story, a lie, a fabrication. He understood why she hadn't done anything—she had no memory of the night, no proof of who was involved. That she had gone to the frat party a virgin and left forever changed, however, was indisputable.

"We need to follow the money," he'd told Jessica. "And that, I am pretty damn good at."

It had not taken Worth long to find the name of the foundation that had awarded the mysterious and sizable grant to Kristina: The Exagorà Group. The word meant nothing to him, and none of the three trustees listed online bore that surname. There was so little information available that he decided to fly out west and do some digging in person. A reputable foundation should have a website with contact information. It was as if this foundation existed solely to benefit Kristina. There was no evidence of any actions taken before her, or since.

Skip had been helpful, finding an old photo on social media of the same three men playing golf together: Clarence O'Day, Everett Barrows, and Todd Bailey, Sr. From there, he'd pieced together the names of their respective sons who had attended the same college as Kristina. They'd all played on the golf team and all belonged to the same fraternity. "I'd bet money they were at the party that night and know something," he'd said, almost shaking with anger. He had a sister. The thought of her going through what this young woman had endured…

That afternoon, Worth boarded the plane and took his seat in first class. He would combine a magazine-related meeting with inquiries into the elusive Exagorà Group. "Hello, Rebecca!" he greeted the petite flight attendant warmly. "Since when do you fly *this* route?"

"I was so pleased to see your name on the manifest." Rebecca smiled. "It's been a while. How is marriage treating you?" Rebecca had been on the first flight Worth and Jessica had taken to Boston together.

Worth beamed. "It's treating me so well that I'm going to be a father."

"Congratulations! Can I get you anything?"

Soon the plane was in the air. Worth rested his eyes and leaned his head against the window. The flight would be seven hours, so a nap would be helpful. The seat next to him was vacant, and for once, he was glad of the solitude. Ordinarily, he enjoyed meeting new people and learning about them, but today he was tired.

Other passengers around him chatted or sipped complimentary champagne. The passenger behind him talked the loudest, conversing with an older woman across the aisle from Worth. He didn't recognize the language, so the words quickly blended with the white noise of the engine, lulling him to sleep.

And then, a gentle tap on his shoulder woke him. Worth looked up to see the man behind him standing. "Would you mind if I take the seat beside you for just a few minutes?" he asked in accented English. He pointed to the woman across the aisle. "She's a little hard of hearing, and that way, I don't have to speak so loudly."

"Of course."

Worth closed his eyes again as the man settled in the wide seat and resumed his conversation. *What language is that?* He and his mother had traveled to most of the major countries, but he couldn't place it. Armenian, maybe?

Suddenly, he heard a word he recognized. *Exagorà.* The man beside him had pulled a Bible out of his pocket and was pointing to a page. There it was again. Exagorà. Worth nudged the man with his elbow.

"Pardon me."

"Yes? What is it, sir? Are we disturbing you?"

Worth sat up. "Not at all. I heard you say a particular word several times that I came across recently. I don't recognize the language. What does 'Exagorà' mean?"

The man smiled broadly. "It is Greek! *I* am Greek! This lady is as well. I am a reader at my church and was sharing some words of comfort with her, as her sister has fallen ill. Exagorà. Means 'redemption'."

"Redemption. Thank you. Please, carry on." Worth closed his eyes once again. *Redemption. For what?*

Eleanor Rigby

Tina was wide awake by the time Chip knocked on her door. She had stayed up well into the night, comparing progress reports. She and the rest of the ESE team were seeing significant progress with the class, but she was always hoping for more. The other teacher had encouraged her to keep a bit of emotional distance. 'Otherwise, you may burn out, and we don't want to lose you.' She knew it was good advice. Elizabeth had encouraged her along the same lines. Mindfulness, codependency—she'd learned a whole different vocabulary in therapy.

Tina greeted Chip with a steaming mug of coffee, the way they both liked it, with cream and sugar, hoping that he would have gotten over whatever seemed to be between them at the end of their evening.

"The old lady's on her way," he said by way of a 'good morning', sitting comfortably in one of the rocking chairs on the porch. It was an odd day when Chip and Tina didn't spend some time this way, sitting together on either her porch or his.

"Hmm," Tina murmured as she settled into the other chair. For someone who had never had a friend to simply *be* with, this was quite the novelty. She was relieved that a good night's sleep seemed to have taken care of whatever burr was up his butt, as he would say. She shivered. "Is it always this cold in September? I guess I'll warm up when we start hauling the old lady's things for her, but I'll need a jacket if she doesn't get here soon."

Chip gazed out into the woods across the road. Squirrels were busily at work, scrambling to find nuts. The leaves had barely started to turn. "Never," he said emphatically. "I'm sixty-four, and I've never seen it this cold, this early. The Almanac warned of it, but I didn't half believe it. 'Should've known better. I guess Mother Nature showed *me* a thing or two."

"Do you get much snow here?" Chip had told her that growing up in the sand hills, it snowed only sporadically each winter.

"Most years, we get one or two good snows, enough to close school down for a few days. With all these mountains, there are tall drifts in some places. I'm gonna cut firewood after we're done with the old lady. I'll leave you and her and me plenty, then work on supplying Mr. Bill's other tenants."

Tina stopped rocking to turn in her chair and face Chip. He was dressed for work, in overalls that were so worn in places that holes threatened. He had on his usual lace-up work boots and a plaid flannel shirt. He had shaved this morning, no doubt to make the best impression on the new tenant. He smelled faintly of Old Spice, which made Tina smile. Her father had used Old Spice. Chip was a handsome man. *But really. Francine? He must be so lonely.* "How many tenants does the eccentric Mr. Cameron have, anyway?"

Chip shook his head with a smirk. "You don't like him, do you? Never even met him. I ask you, is that fair? I didn't make up my mind about you till I met you face-to-face. And we're both prepared to fall in love with the old lady, aren't we, sight unseen? What spur's up your saddle with Mr. Bill?"

Tina shrugged and wrinkled her nose. "I guess you're right. The fact of the matter is… I don't really like men in general. Well, it's true! I didn't have enough time to get to know my father. My grandfather was a wonderful man but not what you'd call communicative or affectionate." She paused, unsure how much she was ready to divulge. "Some *things* happened at college that put me off the whole lot of you." Tina flashed a smile. "But you charmed me, right off the bat, Chip Murphy. I can't remember when I let a man get this close to me, talking like this. I guess my brother-in-law Keith would be the closest, but we only talk when my sister's around."

Chip nodded with some degree of gravity. *Things.* He hoped there was nothing to spoil Mr. Bill's plan, but then again, maybe that would be for the best. He had unreasonably high standards for Ian's would-be woman, in his opinion. It would be a relief to Chip if Tina didn't pass muster. *Then you could have her all to yourself,* his conscience chided. *She's the daughter you never had, fool. Would you be planning all this for your daughter?* Back and forth, the conflicting thoughts raced through his mind.

He was quiet a moment, regaining control. Then he grinned. "'Good thing I've still got a little charm up my sleeve."

A car, followed by a U-Haul truck, stirred up dust as it came around the bend in the gravel road. "Speaking of sleeves, better roll yours up. The old lady's here!" Tina took his coffee mug. "I'll set these inside and be right over."

Chip walked briskly to the drive and directed traffic. Car to the left, truck backed into the middle so there would be less walking to do. He met the drivers, brothers the old lady had apparently babysat long ago and who would do anything for her. It crossed his mind that this was the first time four black folks had been in Poplar Gap at the same time in quite a spell, but he said nothing.

He was not prepared for the old lady, but he managed to stop himself from out-and-out gawking. It was not easy.

One of the brothers opened the car door and offered a hand to help his passenger out. A slender black woman who might have been a tribal queen stepped into the yard. Her white hair was cut very short. When she took off a stylish pair of sunglasses, her big brown eyes almost disappeared when she smiled. She wore a yellow wool suit with a bright scarf at her neck, perfectly setting off mahogany skin that was unlined and silky. She looked more like sixty than eighty. *Uh-oh*, thought Chip. *I may be in trouble now.*

"Eleanor Rigby," she said, extending a manicured hand.

Chip smiled as he shook it, resisting the impulse to take it and raise it to his lips. "Like the song?"

"Like the song, only older and not as lonely," Eleanor said with a soft laugh, as if she got asked the question often.

Tina jogged over, almost tripping over Blue, who had sensed activity in the vicinity from his spot under the porch and come to offer advice. Tina shook Eleanor's hand with wide eyes as she glanced sideways at Chip, mouthing the words '*old lady?*'

"So you're my neighbors!" Eleanor said. "Very pleased to meet you. These boys are Clyde and Cleetus. They were kind enough to drive me, and we've all been up for hours. I hope you're here to help."

Cleetus unhooked the back of the U-Haul and let down the ramp to ease in the unloading, already at work. Clyde gave Tina and Chip a little nod as he turned to join his brother on the truck.

Eleanor continued, looking around with obvious joy. "I've been living in Chapel Hill for ages, but I missed the mountains. 'Thought I'd come back and see who might still be around. Probably not many, but we'll see."

Chip excused himself to help the brothers. As Tina and Eleanor walked into the house, Tina asked how long she'd been gone. "We left when I was fifteen," the woman explained wistfully. "Growing up, I never thought I'd leave. Then I never thought I'd return. But Poplar Gap was always home, you know? Oh! What lovely flowers! And that view out the kitchen window. I swanny, it looks just like what I remember seeing from my kitchen when I was a child."

Tina raised her eyebrows. "I Suwanee? Like the river?"

Eleanor laughed. "I'm well educated, young lady, but I'm also Appalachian born and bred. A lot of our phrases hearken back to Old English. 'I swanny' is a derivative of 'I'll warrant ye'. I swear, in other words, which Mama would've never tolerated, by the way. Very strict, both of my parents. How about yours?"

Tina took a box from Clyde marked "dishes" and set it on the kitchen counter to unpack as Eleanor pointed to her choice of cabinet. "My parents died in a car accident out west, when my sister and I were young, but our mother's parents, our grandparents, raised us. They adopted us, too. Edwards was *their* name."

Eleanor seemed intent on something outside the window. "Adoptive parents must have an awful lot of love to give," she said softly. She gave her head a little shake. "Let's see if we can't speed those men up, shall we? Oh, it's so good to be back. And the house is lovely, don't you think?"

The women chatted easily as they teased and joked with the men doing the heavy lifting. Unlike Tina's, the house was completely bare, or had been, before the men brought in what looked to be expensive antiques. When Tina complimented Eleanor's taste in furniture, the woman beamed. "My parents owned an antique store in Chapel Hill, which I inherited. I sold it this summer—there were some hiccups at the end, which kept delaying my move."

"Your children didn't want to run it?" Tina said, instantly wishing she could take the words back.

Eleanor bit her lip and closed her eyes, quickly recovering. "No, honey. I only had one son and he… didn't want the store."

There's a story there, for sure, Tina thought. *I'll bet he's a handsome thing, with a mother like Eleanor.* The woman moved gracefully through the house, directing the men in a quiet voice while making her preferences clearly known.

With all three men working efficiently, the truck was unloaded in record time. Eleanor joined the brothers outside, to give them one last hug and thank them again. When she handed a fat envelope of cash to them, though, they tried to protest.

"Oh, take it," Eleanor said. "You boys mean the world to me, and it's the least I can do. Drive safe—and I'd love it if you'd let me know when you get back." She stood in the yard, waving as they got into the truck. "Come visit!" she called. "Bring those babies to come see Aunt 'Nor, you hear me?"

Eleanor wiped a tear from her cheek as she walked back inside. "I think the temperature's dropped ten degrees since we got here," she called to the back, where Chip and Tina were putting together the bedstead. "I don't remember it being this chilly this time of year."

Chip scooted the intricately carved headboard to the wall and motioned to Tina to help him with the foundation. "No, ma'am, Miz Rigby. This is *frightful* cold for September. I'll bring wood later today, but I checked the central system and everything's working. Mr. Bill had all his houses upgraded a few years back. Before that, they had window units and oil heaters."

Eleanor stood erect in the bedroom doorway. Although the floor plan was a little different, her home was about the same size as Tina's and Chip's. She had brought too much with her, but that was okay. Better to have too much than too little, she always said. "You can drop the 'Miz Rigby' right now," putting up a hand in anticipation, "and no Miz Eleanor, either! Just plain ole' Eleanor for me."

Tina liked this woman already. As Chip went to another room to fetch the box of linens, she asked, "The song came out in the 60s, so you weren't named for—"

Eleanor flipped her hand in dismissal. "Oh, law, no. Rigby's my married name. And it gets worse. My mother named me for the first lady. I was Eleanor Roosevelt Bradshaw. Eleanor *Rigby* was a happy substitution, even if the marriage was anything but."

Tina was impressed by Eleanor's openness. They were strangers, really, but it appeared the woman was an open book. *I can learn a lot from her, I think.* "How long were you married, if you don't mind my asking?"

Chip returned with the box, which Eleanor opened as Tina and Chip adjusted the mattress. She chatted easily as they helped her put the sheets on the bed, then waited while she found a beautiful hand-crocheted comforter to lay on top. "Not long. *Too* long. My parents arranged it, sort of. I was young. He wasn't."

She straightened up and made a face. "I spent most of my free time crocheting this thing. It didn't take all that long," she said dryly. "He spent *his* free time tom-catting all over Orange County." She smirked at their expressions. "I never had a chance to thank those ladies, either. He was discreet; I'll give him that. Until one of the ladies' husbands caught him with his pants down. Literally. The buckshot got infected."

Tina and Chip weren't sure whether to look sad or not. Eleanor certainly didn't.

"I think I was the youngest widow in the county. Maybe the whole state." Then she laughed heartily. "You too look so solemn! I appreciated the man's enthusiasm, but trust me— there wasn't much to mourn when he was gone."

The tale continued into the afternoon, between directions

for picture placement and which curtains hung where. Eleanor's family had moved from Poplar Gap when she was just a teenager, one of only a few black families in the region at the time. Chapel Hill afforded more opportunities for her father, she said, but he'd gone deep into debt in a matter of months. "Mr. Rigby was more than happy to help him out financially. Guess what his stipulation was?"

Tina was aghast. "Your own father pimped you out to that horrible man?"

Eleanor unwrapped a crystal lamp and set it carefully on a beautiful marble-top table. "It sounds worse than it was." She frowned. "No, it doesn't. That was a terrible thing to do, marrying off a sixteen-year-old to a man older than my father, just to settle a gambling debt. Fortunately, Mr. Rigby had an appetite for rich white women. After a few weeks, he never even… oh, now I've gone and shocked you. I'm sorry."

Chip cleared his throat. "Is this cabinet in the right place, Eleanor? I think it's ready for the china and crystal."

6

October Chill

"**D**id you have a nice day?" Eleanor called from her porch as Tina got out of the car.

"Very nice, thank you." She walked over to join the woman, snuggled under a quilt in the swing with a book on her lap. "What are you reading?"

"*Run with the Horseman*," Eleanor said, holding up the paperback. "Ferrol Sams was a doctor and a writer, and his trilogy is based on his own life. So well written. He grew up between the World Wars. His father had many *nigras* who worked for him. Hard to think back to those dark days, but my parents could tell horror stories. This was in Georgia, but North Carolina had some grim days too."

"May I join you?"

Eleanor lifted the edge of the quilt and laid it on Tina's lap as she settled in. They swung lazily back and forth for a time, enjoying the afternoon sun. Mid-October, the leaves had peaked and fallen already. They could see their breath when they spoke.

"How bad was it around here, in Poplar Gap?"

Eleanor smiled. "Not bad here, at all. The Camerons were

a loyal bunch. Here since the Revolution, and they welcomed anyone who could make a go of it, Indian, poor, escaped slaves. Then later, during Jim Crow, when the Klan really geared up in the state, the Camerons scared them off too."

"So maybe *Mr. Bill* deserves a little more Christian charity than I've been feeling toward him," Tina grunted.

Eleanor smiled and looked across to the woods. "He does indeed."

"Did you know him when you were growing up?" Several months of paying rent through Chip, and she still hadn't met the man. He could have two heads, for all she knew.

Eleanor drew in a breath and let it out. "I did."

"Well. What was he like? No one will tell me anything, other than that he's a good landlord and helps the community and doesn't like people."

Eleanor chuckled softly. "When I knew him, he liked people just fine. His family lived down here then, not on the mountain. We had a one-room schoolhouse that his mother taught in, and we'd take time off to help out at home with chores. It was very casual, very small, very tight-knit. Amazing, really, for its day, inclusive, tolerant. Nothing like in the cities back then. It was just a handful of families. Francine's folks, for one. Ours. Will's."

Tina made a little noise. "Will?"

Eleanor sighed. "Bill. I knew him as Will Cameron. Tall and straight, a Scotsman straight out of a Robert Burns poem. Well, a Scots *boy*. He was fifteen when we left, same age as me."

"Hmm. Interesting. I was always Kristina, or Kris for short, until I moved here. The day I arrived, I met Chip, and on the spur of the moment, I told him to call me Tina. New place, new name, fresh start. I wonder if something happened to Will that made him want to be a different person, live a different life. He didn't leave here, anyway. Chip mentioned once that he married a girl from over the mountain and they had a son."

"So I've heard," Eleanor said curtly. She pushed the quilt aside and stood up. "I think I've had enough fresh air for one afternoon. I think I'll crank up the fireplace tonight and enjoy a pleasant evening alone."

Tina folded the quilt and offered to take it inside, but Eleanor took it from her instead. "Yes. A fire will be nice," Tina said, hoping that an invitation to join her was forthcoming. It was not.

"See you tomorrow, perhaps," Eleanor said and went inside, leaving Tina on the porch alone.

As she got her things from the car, she thought, *she must not have liked Will that much, for all her compliments. That's when she got a little chilly, and it wasn't the temperature.* Tina smiled as she closed the door. She never even locked her car any more, and with Eleanor and Chip—and Blue—nearby, she sometimes didn't even lock her doors. For her, it was almost symbolic, giving herself to the mountains, to her new friends, with no need to lock them out. True, she hadn't told them anything specific about her college trauma, but perhaps in time. For now, her small class was delightful and challenging. She was always learning new ways to guide her students.

One boy in particular, a teenager, was adamant. "Autism doesn't define me, Miss Tina. I can do anything I want." Jeffrey, quite bright, diagnosed with what they called HFA, or high-functioning autism.

"His parents divorced over him," her co-teacher Martha had said quietly as the children painted one afternoon. "Dad wanted to fix Jeffrey, find a cure, blame somebody. Mom accepted him as he is, embraced the new normal when he was diagnosed." They stood watching the young man carefully work. Everything he did was meticulous.

Jeffrey Wilson inspired her, as did the ever-positive Martha, the aide, and the other students. Every day held new inspiration for her to grow and mature. It had taken a few months, but she had everything she needed. A cozy house, a shower, thermal curtains to keep the winter at bay, a healthy stockpile of firewood, good friends, a new bed. *A twin bed*, she thought suddenly. She had a vision of Eleanor's four-poster with its wide goose-down mattress. How lovely it would be to sprawl on a Saturday morning, stretch out, cat-like, in all directions, knowing the day stretched out ahead, full of new adventures.

Even lovelier would be to have a man curled beside me.

The thought, unbidden, shocked her to her core. Maybe she should call Elizabeth. She didn't want a man. She didn't need a man. *Is this what happens? You crack open the door just enough to let in a few friends, only to become needy?*

She'd grown comfortable spending time with Eleanor and Chip. Often, they would play cards in the evening or grab dinner at Francine's. Francine had been in the first grade when Eleanor moved but thought she remembered her babysitting. "I thought your name was Nora, though."

Tina was watching Eleanor's face as they had chatted and given Francine their orders, a few weeks earlier. She'd smiled and nodded. "A few people called me that, yes. But Mama liked Eleanor better."

Eleanor had obviously not wanted her company that evening, though, and Chip was God only knew where, probably bowing and scraping before King Bill. Co-workers had their own families; most of them lived closer to the school or on the other side of the mountain. She was fine by herself. Frowning, she walked inside and laid her things down on the little dining table. Walking down the hallway, she looked out the window of the back door, squinting her eyes at Chip's porch and yard. Even Blue was making himself scarce.

"Hey, Chip," Tina called from the back porch. She had hung out some towels to dry, only to find them frozen stiff. "I guess this wasn't the best idea."

Chip was raking leaves from the big oak that stood between their yards, bundled in a knit hat, overcoat and gloves. There were no fences—Blue and the other neighbors' dogs and cats roamed freely, minding their own business and exploring the woods at will. He dropped his rake and walked closer. "Leave 'em be. The sun will thaw them out directly." Little puffs of air were visible as he talked. "What's the temperature this morning? I'm guessing, oh, twenty-eight degrees?"

Tina checked the gauge tacked to the porch post. "Spot on, as usual."

"You been doing okay? I've been so busy lately, we haven't talked much. You ever go exploring? 'Bout too cold now."

Tina's heart leapt. She was beginning to think both he and Eleanor had tired of her, or she'd said something wrong, was still too much of a city girl for their tastes. Maybe they really *were* just busy. She knew Eleanor had had guests—Cleetus and Clyde had come with their families on separate weekends, but it had gotten so cold, they'd stayed indoors.

"I thought maybe you were avoiding me."

Chip laughed, studying a patch of frost in the brown grass. "Not at all, not at all. Mr. Bill's had me running him all over the place. Some lawyer in Asheville, an office over in Tennessee. Says he wants to get his affairs in order." The words brought a frown to his face.

"Is he okay? I guess I understand him staying away if he's unwell. He's such an enigma."

"Enig-what? Mr. Bill is white, you know that?" Chip's eyes were twinkling now.

At first, Tina's eyes were wide, embarrassed that he thought she'd used a slur, then realized he was teasing. "You." She threw a stiff washcloth at him, which he caught. "It's just that half the time you make him sound like a giant of superhuman strength and power, and the other half this frail old man you have to cart around."

Chip nodded. "Yep. I can see how you'd be confused. I guess he's a giant to me, anyway. Done so much for us here. Things most folks don't even know. But," he stepped closer to the porch and lowered his voice, "he's the smartest man I know, and he's convinced he's not long for this world."

Tina's concern was genuine. "Oh! But he's up there all alone on the mountain. What if he dies? How long before anyone knew? That's awful, Chip. I had no idea. He could stay in my spare room, if you don't have one. An old man—"

Chip held up a hand to stop her. "Don't you worry your pretty little head another second. Humph. I'm not even sure he's right—seems healthy as a horse to me, but he's stubborn as a dadblame *mule*. But he's not alone, so that's okay. He's gotten awfully quiet, though. Cart him around all day and might get four words out of him the whole time. Lot on his mind, he says. And he's eighty. Hardly seems *old*."

Tina leaned on the porch post and sighed. "I was sure he'd want to come see Eleanor. They must have been in school together."

"I thought so, but he says he don't remember any Eleanor Rigby. Or any Rigbys at all."

Tina giggled. "That was her married name. Oh! I think you were out of the room when she told me her given name. I asked about the Beatles song, you know, Eleanor Rigby, picks up the rice in the church where a wedding has been…"

Chip sat down on the porch and clapped his hands for Blue to join him. The dog scooted on his belly from under Chip's porch and bounded across the yard to his master for a good ear scratching. "You've got a nice voice, Tina. I always loved the Beatles."

Tina sat beside him, rubbing Blue's silky back. "Me too.

Anyway, I asked her about her name, and she said she'd been Eleanor Roosevelt Bradshaw. Mr. Rigby gave her a name and not a whole hell of a lot more until he died and left her a pile of money."

"Hmph. Mr. Bill never asks about his tenants, leaves that all up to me. E. Rigby, K. Edwards—that's you, of course, even though now you want to be T. Edwards. I pick up the rent checks, cash them, take him the money maybe once a month. He calls now and then for this or that. But I had nothing much when I moved here, and he's been awfully good to me. I think the world of him. Not much for conversation, but I guess you get that way living on a mountain."

Tina sat up straight, stretching her back. Jeffrey often reminded her to stand up straighter, she thought with a smile. Such a stickler for meticulous posture, like everything else about him. "But you said he's not alone? I thought his wife died?"

Chip nodded, grateful that his darker skin covered the heat of his sudden blush. "I thought you knew. Didn't I ever tell you about his grandson?"

Tina made a face. "No? I thought he was just a hermit living up there by himself, hating the world. You never told me what happened to make him that way. He married and had a son. Lives on a mountain. That's about it! I filled in the blanks —a son would've grown up and moved away. You never said a word about a grandson. How old is he?"

Chip rubbed his chin. His winter beard was taking its time coming in, but there was salt-and-pepper fuzz all over his face. It itched. Or maybe the conversation was making him squirmy. "Oh," he began vaguely, "I don't rightly know. About your age, I reckon."

Tina raised her eyebrows. "And?"

"What? Let's see. His name is Ian."

"And? I swear, this is like pulling teeth. It's too cold for this.

I'm going inside. Want some coffee? Fresh pot." Tina stood up slowly, awkward in all the layers she'd put on. "You sure these towels will be dry sometime in the near future?"

Chip stood and started walking back for the rake, talking over his shoulder. "I'm sure. But no, got a pot inside already." He stopped. "You never did answer my question. About your explorations."

Tina brushed some grass and dog hair from her jeans' legs. "Not yet, no." She gazed up at the clear blue sky. "I've got some reading to do for school today, but thanks for the reminder. I think I'll take a drive tomorrow."

"Want some company? Blue and me got the whole day free."

"Maybe another time. I don't have a timetable. I might end up over the mountain at a fabric store, for all I know." She grinned, knowing full well Chip's opinion of fabric stores.

Chip gave a little bow. "Understood. Those things suck the lifeblood right out of a man. You go on, then." He watched as she returned his wave and went inside. He'd been waiting for the opportunity, and this was it.

7

The Planning

The moon was a waxing sliver in the sky that evening, with cloudy skies besides. Very cloudy. If it warmed up just a hair, Chip thought, it might snow. The woolly worms were very thick. A flock of geese had flown over that afternoon, honking very low in the sky. That might mean bad weather coming. Well, Mr. Bill wanted what he wanted, whether the weather held or not.

Stealthily, Chip walked across his yard and around Tina's house, the frost crunching under his boots. He'd put Blue inside and brought some tools. Crouching behind Tina's SUV, he felt underneath for the gas tank and then pulled a nail from his pocket. *This shouldn't make too much noise.* And who would hear him? Both Tina and Eleanor would be sound asleep at this hour.

As quietly as possible, Chip opened the door and turned the spare key he knew she kept in the console, just enough to check the gas gauge. Half full. *Not enough she'll fill it up before, but it might be empty by morning.* Clumsy, but he'd run out of time. He put the key back and closed the door quietly, just until the light went off. *Blue would be howling if he saw me out here.*

Holding the nail against the tank with one hand, he tapped it one time, then pulled the nail out with his pliers. The fuel began to drip onto the gravel, steadily but slowly. If Tina had let him go along, he could've suggested they take his truck, stay in control. This was riskier, but Mr. Bill was impatient, and this was his first real opportunity. He couldn't press her, or she might've gotten suspicious. She was pretty smart. *And pretty.* If Ian didn't like her… no. She thought of him like a father, and that was so flattering, it drove any other thoughts from his mind.

Satisfied that she'd either wake up to an empty tank and ask him for a ride, or run out of gas where he could "rescue" her, Chip walked back to his house and lay down on top of his bed, coat and all. Kidnapping a girl might be harder than he'd anticipated. *I just hope she can forgive me,* he thought, drifting off to sleep.

Early the next morning, Eleanor was walking up the road when Tina went out to her car. *I hope I have that much energy when I'm her age.* "Ready for something hot to drink, I'll bet!" she called to the woman. Eleanor, after that first day, had been less forthcoming but mostly friendly. A few times, there had been a chill, like a little wall had gone up, for whatever reason. Tina tried not to worry about it, reminding herself to be mindful, as Elizabeth had taught her. 'Observe what's going on as if in a mirror, so it doesn't affect you so deeply.' *Good advice if I'd just do it.*

"Absolutely." Eleanor approached her, looking up at the sky. "I think it's warmed up just a hair, but look at those clouds. They look mean, don't they?"

Tina frowned at her car door. She must not have shut it all the way yesterday. "Chip keeps warning it's going to be a bad winter. I guess he'd know." She slipped into the driver's seat.

"I'm off to explore—haven't really taken the time since I got here, you know."

"Enjoy! Come over for cards later if you want to. I've got church, then a nap, but if you're back around three, I could give you that crochet lesson you asked about." Eleanor shook her head. "No, I'm out of yarn. I donated all my odd pieces to the church last week. They're making ornaments for the Christmas bazaar." Eleanor's church was ten miles away, close to Tina's school. She'd asked her to join her plenty of times, but Tina had always bowed out. Driving that far every day was enough. Weekends, she needed to relax.

And now you're going for a Sunday drive. "If the fabric store's open in Humphrey, I could pick some up."

Eleanor laughed, holding the handle of the SUV. "Honey, this is rural North Carolina. *Everything* closes on Sunday. Maybe you could pick some up after work this week? Have a nice day." She closed the door with a little slam and waved as Tina pulled out of the driveway.

She was still standing there, enjoying the crisp October air when she heard Chip's truck start up. She watched him drive off with Blue beside him and waved, but he didn't see her. Eleanor took a deep breath. Instead of the expected woodsy smell of clean mountain air, there was something different. Something pungent. Not unpleasant, but…

Eleanor noticed a discolored area of gravel where Tina usually parked. It was too far back and not the right smell or color for oil. She stooped down and touched a wet piece of gravel, holding it to her nose. It brought back memories of old-time filling stations and helping her father with the lawnmower. Gasoline. She looked down the road with concern. A gas leak could be serious.

Pulling her cell phone from her coat pocket, she punched in Tina's number. The SUV had all the bells and whistles, she knew. The Bluetooth would pick up the call.

"Hey!" Tina was surprised at the call. "Everything okay?"

"It's probably nothing, but there's a little puddle of gas on your driveway. What should your gas gauge say?"

She heard Tina groan. "I had at least a half a tank, and now it's almost empty. I didn't even look when I got in the car. Ugh."

"How far have you gone? I saw Chip leave just after you, and he's probably on the mountain road headed for the Camerons'. If you go that way, maybe you can catch up to him. He always carries a can with him."

"Okay," Tina sighed. "Thanks for the head's up. Wish me luck!" She pressed the button on the steering wheel to end the call and groaned. "I don't even know where the dadblame mountain road is!" she yelled. *Dadblame Chip. Now I'm talking like him.*

Everyone knew where Cameron Mountain was, of course. She'd just head that way and hope for the best. *Already running on fumes, probably. How much below the fill line can you go?* There! Off to the right, there was a road. Paved, even. Tina recognized Chip's paint job on small signs attached every ten feet of so to an electric fence, "*Keep out. Danger.*" *Yeah, I'm in danger of running out of gas.* She wondered if there were bears this time of year.

Chip's truck was nowhere in sight. She'd climbed a good bit in elevation, when just around a sharp bend, the engine sputtered and died. *Damn.* She tried calling Chip, chiding herself for not calling sooner. No bars. Tina grabbed her heavy coat from the back seat and wrapped a woolen scarf around her neck. *Gloves, gloves.* She pulled them from the glove compartment. *So that's why they call it that.*

She began to walk up the steep road. *Mindfulness. Look at life as if in a mirror so it doesn't affect you.* The ache in her calves would be hard to ignore, she thought wryly. She thought briefly about heading down the mountain rather than up, but if Chip really had come this way, he had to be above her. And if he hadn't, maybe she could find her way to wherever in the hell "Mr. Bill" lived before a bear chewed her up and spat her out.

She'd walked for about thirty minutes when she rounded a turn and fairly shrieked with relief. Chip's truck was parked on a narrow shoulder on the mountain side of the road. Chip and Blue were standing on the other side of the road, looking down into the deep ravine.

"Man, am I glad to see you!" She huffed and puffed to join him.

Instead of answering her, Chip held a finger to his lips and pointed below. An enormous black bear was maybe a hundred yards away, ambling slowly closer.

"Shouldn't we get in the truck?" Tina whispered. Beside her, every muscle in Blue's taut body was tense, ready to spring into action.

"Steady, boy," Chip murmured. "She's not botherin' anybody."

As they watched, the bear sniffed the air and looked up at them before turning to head in a different direction. Tina let out the breath she hadn't realized she was holding and squeezed Chip's arm. "Oh my! If you weren't here, I would have been terrified." She pointed down the road. "I ran out of gas."

Chip nodded. "I figured there was a reason you were on foot," he said with more good cheer than he felt.

Tina shook her head. "I should've checked this morning. Eleanor smelled the gas from a leak and called me. She's the one who suggested I see if you were on this road, which was fortuitous."

Chip was silent. He'd made it a point to call Eleanor and tell her he planned to go to Cameron Mountain this morning. Good thing he did.

"So, do you have a gas can?" Tina's nose was runny from the cold air. "Fill me up, and I'll be on my way."

"Well, I need to see Mr. Bill first, and you can finally meet him. On the way back, we'll check out your car."

Tina didn't have much choice, but she was excited about meeting the man Chip idolized. If Mr. Cameron really was sickly, who knew how many opportunities she'd get? "Do you think his grandson, what's-his-name, will be there too?" It was not an unpleasant thought, surprisingly enough. Meeting anyone her age, even a guy, would be novel.

"Ian. Maybe," Chip said as he opened his door and motioned for Tina to get in and slide across. There wasn't room on the passenger side to open the door. Blue jumped in after her. "No tellin'."

The truck drove slowly up, up, up. The road ended well before the mountain did, however. Chip pulled over as far as he could, this time with the mountainside to his left. "Get out. Gotta walk from here."

Muttering, but grateful for his help, Tina held the door open for Blue and Chip and slammed it shut. "I'm certainly getting my exercise today."

Chip was uncharacteristically serious. "Now listen. You follow in my footsteps, you hear? Every step I take, you take. I'll walk slow. Blue knows the way, but you don't."

"What do you mean? There's no path?"

"Of a sort, yes, but there are false paths, too, and bear traps, and traps of other kinds. Mr. Bill is serious about keeping people away, and he's had a long time to work on it."

Tina kept dark thoughts to herself. *Honestly. You'd think there was gold in them thar hills with all this rigmarole.* She was tired, thirsty, and her legs ached. What if the car needs repairing, not just gas? How would she get the car to a shop? Were there even shops around? Suddenly, everything, the move here, this community, Chip, seemed like an exercise in futility. Annoying. "Lead on, Macduff," she quoted.

"Who? Oh. I gotcha." Now that the plan was in play, Chip was more relaxed. "Didn't think I read Shakespeare, did you?"

"Not really. How far is it?"

"Pretty far. You'll have noticed that when I'm gone with Mr. Bill, I'm *gone*, for a while."

The two walked for what seemed like hours but was a fraction of that, with Chip in the lead, stepping carefully in a vaguely serpentine route. Tina followed. Blue took up the rear patiently. Suddenly, the report of a gun was heard in the distance—but not far enough away for Tina's tastes.

"Does he let people hunt up here?"

"Hardly. Maybe Ian's out grubbing for dinner."

Now that he mentioned, it, Tina realized that the sky had grown darker. Daylight, but fading. And the clouds were looking ominous. "Will we be able to make our way back in the dark? I didn't bring my flashlight with me."

Chip didn't turn his head but said, "No worries. Just a little bit more."

8

Trapped

T ina's fatigue did not dampen her amazement as they stepped from dense evergreens into a clearing. A beautiful cabin stood before them. She had expected some kind of dilapidated shack, although now that she thought about it, why *wouldn't* Bill Cameron have money? He was the landlord for at least three tenants and probably many more. She hadn't thought that through.

The log cabin was low to the ground, with a front porch. Firewood was stacked neatly against the nearest side of the cabin. Smoke billowed from a beautiful stone chimney. Lights were on inside.

"Electricity? Way up here?"

Chip nodded as he slowed his pace. Blue, familiar with the place, ran ahead to the porch and scratched at the door. "Cell tower much further up. Mr. Bill's stipulation for giving them permission was that the company run power down to him. Even put septic in. What a job that was! But it sure did make the place more comfortable. That was just a few years ago, too."

As surprised as Tina was by the cabin, the man who

emerged from it had an even greater effect. A tall, lanky man stepped onto the porch, leaving the door ajar.. His thick hair had no doubt been auburn at some point, judging from his fair complexion, but it was white as a cloud now. It matched a full beard that fell perhaps six inches onto his chest. Belying the temperature, he wore a wool shirt and trousers but no coat. When he smiled, all of Tina's annoyance with the man fell away. He looked like someone she would enjoy getting to know.

Tina followed Chip to the porch and then inside. Blue took up what must be a regular spot in front of the fire as Tina looked around. The cabin wasn't spacious, but it was homey and neat. It was also warm enough that she could take off her coat, hat and gloves.

"Here, miss, I'll take those," Bill Cameron said. He hung the coat on a peg near the door alongside other outerwear, stuffing the toboggan and gloves into its pockets. "Can I get you some tea?"

"Y-yes, please," she said shyly. "Mr. Cameron, the house I'm renting from you is very nice. Thank you. And Chip's been very helpful."

"To me as well," the man said as he poured a mug of steaming liquid from a kettle on the wood stove. Kitchen, dining, and living room was all one area. A black bear skin adorned the wood floor in front of the fireplace. A stairway at the other end of the room led to what Tina assumed was a bedroom. There were two closed doors at the back, another leading outside past the kitchen area. Chip motioned for her to sit in a straight rush-bottom chair close to the warmth. He remained standing.

"Your home is beautiful, Mr. Cameron. Did you build it yourself?" The herbal tea was too hot to drink without blowing on it, but although the flavor was not as sweet as she would prefer, it felt good going down.

"I did, thank you. It's held up well. So. Tina. What brings

you here on a fine Sunday afternoon?" Bill handed a mug of tea to Chip before sitting in an upholstered rocker opposite her. His voice was deep and clear.

"I was taking a drive and ran out of gas. Chip rescued me but said we needed to come here first," she said with a smile to Chip. *He's acting so strange. Surely, after all these years, he's not intimidated by this man.* "I've been wanting to meet you, sir." She couldn't help adding, "I'd thought you might come down to meet us."

"Us?" Bill frowned slightly. "I thought you lived alone."

"I do." Tina felt as if she were at a job interview that wasn't going as well as she'd hoped. He seemed friendly, but… "I meant Eleanor. Eleanor Rigby." She giggled nervously. "Like the song, but not. I thought you might want to get reacquainted, since she used to live here."

Bill shook his head dismissively. "I told Chip, I don't remember any Rigbys, and no Eleanors, either. There are a lot of small communities in the mountains. And she's older, yes? Maybe she's just a little confused." He sighed. "It happens. Time catches up with us, whether we want it to or not."

You look healthy to me. "She was a Bradshaw. And she went by Nora, I think. Said her mother preferred Eleanor."

Bill closed his eyes and rested his head. He was silent for so long, she thought he might have gone to sleep, but finally, he inhaled deeply and sat up. "Nora Bradshaw is my new tenant? You've met her? Is she well?"

Are those tears? I knew *there was more to her story.* "She's very well. And very beautiful, too. I'm surprised Chip didn't mention that to you."

Bill smirked a little. "Oh, he raved about the beauty of E. Rigby and tried to get me to meet her, maybe ask her out. But I gave my heart to one woman a very long time ago, and I've not been much interested since then. Nora Bradshaw, however, that may be a different matter."

Tina nodded, looking at the flames. "I heard about your wife, Mr. Cameron. And your son and his wife. I'm sorry for your loss. I lost my parents when I was a child. It doesn't get easier, does it?"

Bill cleared his throat and shot a look at Chip, who shrugged an apology. Clearly, Chip had disclosed more than was appreciated about his boss' personal life. "No, but we get better at it. Did Chip also tell you that I have a grandson?"

"Yes, sir." Tina's eyes drifted to the upstairs. "Is he here? I'd like to meet him. Chip said we were about the same age, and as you may not be aware, there are not a lot of us in that demographic in Poplar Gap."

"I see Chip was quite talkative about some details but secretive on others. And that's fine. I'm glad that you're finally here." He leaned forward in his chair. "My family's been in Poplar Gap for hundreds of years. Hundreds. Think of it! I can trace the Camerons back to before the Revolutionary War. Some of us settled in the middle of the state, some on the coast. My branch came to the mountains, where we stayed. Towns have sprung up and died, communities have withered as the children grew up to head for the cities, but the Cameron name has been constant here."

There didn't seem to be anything to say, so Tina just sipped her tea. *He's watching me so intently.* "What kind of tea is this?"

Bill frowned. "It's my own blend. Herbs from around here. Most people like it better with a little honey."

"I'd like to try that, please."

Bill took the mug from her, refilled it and stirred honey from a Ball jar on the shelf above the stove. "I'm eighty, young lady. I've learned to ask for what I want. You should do that too."

"Yes, sir," she said quietly. *This guy should get with Elizabeth! They'd have a blast together.*

Bill began to pace around the room slowly. "Ian's hunting,

but he should be back by dark. I'd hoped, well, things haven't gone exactly as I hoped." He glared at Chip. "I'd hoped you might meet before now, but it didn't work out. I had to get some things done; you had things to do. And now that you're here, I find I have a surprising priority I hadn't anticipated. Chip, can you take me down? I want to speak with Mrs. Rigby."

Chip cleared his throat and tried to avoid Tina's questioning eyes. "Sure thing, Mr. Bill. Just leave Tina here for now and pick her up when I bring you back?"

"Just take me wi—"

"That'll be fine," Bill said. He turned to Tina. "You can relax for a few hours. Ian will be back soon, and you can visit with him. My business with Mrs. Rigby shouldn't take long."

The traveling back and forth will, though. The nerve of this guy. "I'd rather leave with you and meet Ian later, if you don't mind."

Bill took a heavy coat from one of the pegs and put it on, pulling a wool balaclava and leather, fur-lined gloves from a pocket. "Actually, I do. I'm a stubborn man, as I'm sure Chip has told you. And I get what I want. I want you to meet my grandson." He paused, as if unsure how much to say. "To be completely truthful, I want you to marry him. Be with him, anyway. I may not be long for this world, and it's important to me to find a suitable mate for him." He frowned. "A lot of cultures in the world take care of the matchmaking for the young ones, from Biblical times till now. But I suppose it must sound odd to you."

Tina stood up and walked as calmly as she could until she was close enough to the man to smell the scent of wood smoke clinging to his beard. "It sounds *criminal*. Sir, you can't just make me stay here on top of a mountain by myself, in hopes that I'll fall in love with your grandson tonight!"

Bill smiled sadly. "I don't expect you to fall in love. I wasn't in love with my wife. We had some good years, though. My son loved his wife so much that her death tore him apart. That, I understand. I've been in love once myself, long ago. It liked to kill me when she was gone, and I swore I'd never fall in love again. Too painful. Ian's a good man, Miss Edwards, and he can give a good life to the right woman. A *pure* woman. Kind, pretty, smart. Chip here thinks you check all the boxes, and I'd trust him with my life."

Tina suddenly laughed so loudly that it startled both men. She stormed over to the fireplace and waited for her laughter to die down before she whipped around, angry. "Pure? You wanted a *virgin* for your perfect grandson? Boy, did *you* grab the wrong girl."

"Chip." Bill Cameron's voice was almost a growl.

Tina almost felt sorry for her supposed friend. *All this time, he was studying me to make sure I was good enough for precious Mr. Bill and Ian. But he looks more miserable than even* I *would have wished on him.*

Chip uncomfortably shifted his weight from foot to foot. "Mr. Bill, I couldn't ask about that. 'Wouldn't have been proper."

Tina shrieked, "Proper! What in the hell about this scenario could even remotely be described as proper? I want to go home! Now! And you can't stop me." Tina ran for the door, but Bill grabbed her and held her tightly.

"You can't run out into the woods. It isn't safe."

"And this is?" Tina's face was red with anger.

Chip looked at Bill. "If you want to go down, we need to get on. But I know this 'un. She'll run as soon as she can. You shouldn't't've spooked her like that. Why can't we just all sit here and have a nice talk and get to know one another until Ian comes, and then maybe she'll think differently." At the expression on Tina's face, he continued, "Or maybe she won't. But then you'll know she's *not* the one, and we can keep looking. Please, Mr. Bill. Let's just stay here."

Bill Cameron was resolute. He walked into the kitchen area and pulled out a rope from the drawer of a pie safe. "I'm sorry," he said softly. "I don't know how much longer I have. She's here, Ian's here, and I need to see Nora as soon as I can. Her being in Poplar Gap puts a new twist on the matter."

"You *did* know her!" Tina's eyes were round as inspiration dawned. "*She* was your one love?" Her mind was reeling. When the Bradshaws left, it was the early 1950s. It would have been difficult for a mixed race couple, even if they weren't teenagers. Strict parents might force an end to it. *Poor Eleanor.* She was too angry with Bill Cameron to feel any sympathy for him.

Without answering, Bill signaled to Chip, who whispered, "I'm so sorry" as he firmly pinned her arms to her side and led her back to her chair. Bill pulled her hands behind her, at first gently but rougher as she struggled.

"This wasn't the way I thought it'd be, but it's too dangerous for you to be loose, if you'd try to leave. Chip's sure you would."

"You're goddamn right," Tina muttered.

Bill tied the rope into a knot and clucked his tongue disapprovingly. "Impure *and* sacrilegious. Chip, we will talk."

Chip put his coat on and bent down to whisper in Tina's ear. "I'm so sorry, Tina. Really, I am. But I'll be back to get you, don't worry. You'll be safer like this till Ian gets back than if you headed out on the mountain alone. He's dead set on his plans. There's no talking to him when he's like this. I know."

Tina was livid. She hissed without looking at her supposed friend, the father figure she had trusted. "Be sure to do exactly what *Mr.* Bill asks. And when you're done, maybe you can look for a spine." Her heart sank at the words, knowing how they would hurt, but *honestly.* She was tied to a chair because of these clowns.

Chip called for Blue to come with them. Even the dog hung his head low as he passed Tina. With a little headshake of silent apology, Chip reached into her coat and pulled out her cell phone before shutting the door behind them quietly. Tina was alone.

9

Nora Bradshaw, At Your Services

C hip was sullen and silent in the truck as he and Bill Cameron passed Tina's abandoned SUV. "That was a damn nasty thing to do, Mr. Bill," he muttered.

"Yup." He was staring out the window at the sky. "I think we're in for a real storm, Chip." He looked at his driver. "I know you think she's a beauty, but you heard her yourself. She's not pure. And pretty is as pretty does, my mama always said."

"Well my mama would say 'Hell hath no fury like a woman scorned.' You trussed her up and left her. What if something's happened to Ian and she's there for hours 'till we get back? I mean, come on." Chip made disapproving noises in his throat.

"From the looks of that sky, it could be more than that. Are you sure Eleanor Rigby said she was a Bradshaw?"

Chip shook his head. "That's what she said. What she told Tina, and Tina told me. You don't mind trusting her when it suits you, do you?"

Bill Cameron chuckled softly. "You're really riled up, aren't you?"

Chip stole a glance at his boss and friend. "Yup," he said, matching the other's tone perfectly.

They rode in silence for several miles with Blue asleep between them, his big head resting on Bill's lap. Now and then, Bill would give the dog a pat or a scratch. Finally, he let out a long sigh. "I should tell you about it, Chip, before we get there. It may not be pretty."

For the rest of the trip, Bill Cameron told Chip what he had not spoken of in over sixty years—he'd felt obliged to tell his wife everything, or close to it.

William Cameron had fallen in love with Nora Bradshaw as soon as he was old enough to know the difference between boys and girls. He'd grown up around animals, of course, and had seen his share of mating. It wasn't something he thought about; it was just part of nature, part of life. Nora was a playmate, like all the other children his age in Poplar Gap.

Prejudice is taught, not born; Poplar Gap was an odd entity —a little pocket of inclusion and equality that was decades ahead of its time. Its inhabitants liked to stay where they were. They took care of each other, immediately suspicious of outsiders. The Bradshaws were the only black family, descendants of mixed marriages or runaway slaves. No one asked, or cared to.

What was not readily evident is that the Bradshaws themselves were not as tolerant as they appeared, not when it came to their only child. Playing hopscotch and Capture the Flag with little white boys and girls was one thing. Will Cameron holding hands with her and getting caught up in the Bradshaw's hay loft with her half-dressed was something else altogether.

"We were both fifteen. Uncle B, we called him, he didn't bother to sit us down and talk things over. He yanked her up out of the hay, told me to get my skinny white ass off his property, and the next thing I knew, they were gone."

Chip gave a murmur of understanding. Prejudice came in

all colors, he knew. "But so young—don't you think it was just puppy love? I mean, you married later."

Bill's voice was strained with emotion. "It was the real thing, Chip. I never loved anyone but Nora. I would have made her happy if they'd have let me. They just dropped off the earth. I didn't have any money, no car, no way to look for her. About a year later, somebody saw her in Chapel Hill, of all places. And she was married."

"What'd you do? Did you think about going up there and stealing her?" Mr. Bill's apparent tolerance for kidnapping had not escaped Chip's thinking. And he knew, if Mr. Bill didn't, that Eleanor's marriage had been both unhappy and brief.

Bill shook his head. "She made her choice, I reckon. Maybe I *was* just puppy love to her, I don't know. I thought I did. I never heard her married name, though. Had no idea Eleanor Rigby was my Nora."

They were approaching the last leg of the journey. "Did you tell your wife about her?"

"I did, Chip. I tried to be a good husband, and I think Maggie would have told you I was. We had some good times. She was a good woman, good mother. We made a tolerable match, such as it was," Bill said, his voice breaking. "I just had so little to give her. God bless her, she didn't ask for much."

Chip sighed. Marriage was not something he knew about, other than observing others. "So what are you going to do now?"

Bill shook his head, staring out the window in a daze. "Damned if I know. I guess it depends on her. I've been waiting a long time for an explanation, for answers as to why she left. I hope to get that much from her before I die, at least."

Chip's truck pulled into Eleanor's driveway. Even before the engine was turned off, Eleanor ran outside, pulled open the passenger side door, took Bill's face in her hands and kissed him—for all the world, like they were fifteen once again.

The three of them sat in the comfortable little sitting area inside, drinking sassafras tea and eating freshly baked cookies. After the initial, somewhat enthusiastic greeting, Eleanor had grown shy, letting the men do most of the small talk. She was concerned about Tina, of course, but Chip seemed to think that after they visited a spell, he'd take Mr. Bill back up the mountain and bring Tina home.

Outside, the wind began to howl. Snow fell furiously, all at once, on the tin roof of the house. Just that quickly, the weather became a factor. "We'd better leave right now, Mr. Bill," Chip urged. "No tellin' when it will let up."

There was a terrible crash not far away. Even Bill jumped. "Would you go see what that was, Chip? I'll help you get these into the kitchen, Nora. I can visit again tomorrow, if that's all right with you."

As Chip went outside to investigate the noise, Bill followed his long ago love into the kitchen. He stood there, a sad old man holding a delicate cup and saucer in each hand. He felt like a fool, but he had to know. "Why'd you leave me, darlin'?"

Eleanor put her hands on the edge of the sink for support. She'd aged beautifully, Bill thought. He didn't know much about cosmetic surgery, but she was close enough to what he remembered to make him doubt she'd had any "work" done. There were lines, of course. Her hair was white. She was taller, too. *Guess she wasn't fully-grown at fifteen. Neither was I.*

Eleanor began to weep. Filled with remorse, Bill set down the china and wrapped his arms around her. "I'm sorry. You don't have to tell me. You don't owe me anything."

Eleanor looked up at him, tears streaming. "*Owe* you? Don't you think I've wanted to tell you? They *made* me, Will. When Daddy dragged me inside and asked me what was going on, I told him that I was—they packed everything up and hauled me off. He, um, he started to beat me, but Mama stopped him. Told him it would wait till—"

"You told him what? That you were in love with a white boy? That I wanted to marry you just as soon as we were old enough? *What* did you tell him, Nora?" Bill's voice was thick and low.

Eleanor pulled away from his arms and wiped her tears with a lace-trimmed handkerchief from her pocket. She sniffed and straightened her back. She wasn't as tall as he was, but he could tell she was no pushover. "I told my Daddy that I was in love with Will Cameron and that I was carrying his baby."

Bill's knees gave way, but Eleanor reached out for him to help him regain himself, leading him back into the living room to sit on the couch beside her. "You were pregnant? How long? Why didn't you tell me?"

Eleanor's back was straight as a rod, but her head was down, twisting her handkerchief in her hands. "I wasn't sure, Will. I thought so, but I thought if I told Daddy I was, he'd let me marry you. I thought he'd *make* you marry me." She looked at him sadly. "But he didn't want a white grandchild. Half-white. It was that simple. He said Poplar Gap might be okay with it, but he'd be damned if he stayed here all his life with the shame I'd brought on him. We packed up that night, left everything we couldn't take."

"W-were you pregnant?"

Eleanor nodded then looked at him with a smile. "A boy, Will. You gave me a boy."

Tears spilled down Bill's craggy cheeks now. "What happened to him? Is he okay? Can I meet him?"

"Oh, Will," Eleanor said, grasping his hands. "They took him away. I didn't even get to see him." Together, the two of them cried in each other's arms for all the years, all the pain, all the loss.

Chip's boots could be heard stomping on the front porch.

He opened the door. "That was a tree falling, what we heard. We could climb over, but a vehicle won't make it off the road until it's moved. I, um, loaned my chain saw to Mr. Wilbur last week, and he's way over on County Road 10. The snow's *really* coming down. No sign of a let up. Almanac was right on target. Looks like you're bunking with me tonight, boss." He finally noticed that they hadn't even turned when he barged in. "Everything okay?"

Bill wiped his eyes and waved him in. "Sit down, Chip. Might as well loop you in since you heard my side of the story. Time you heard hers."

When he was up to speed, Chip couldn't stop shaking his head. "So you had the baby and they just took him? You don't know what happened to him?"

"I know what happened to *me*, as I already told you. Daddy had opened an antique store, but also discovered a new hobby —gambling. After a few months, Daddy had gone deep into debt to Mr. Rigby," she explained. "He pretty much traded me to the man." She saw the look on Bill's face. "William Cameron, he was thirty years older than I was and a woman-izing son-of-a-bitch who got shot by a jealous husband before I could shoot him myself."

"Did he—"

Eleanor's eyebrows shot up. "What do you think? I was his wife. But—" she glanced at Chip apologetically. "I hope this doesn't shock you." Turning back to Bill, she said, "You and I were amateurs, but we sure did take to the sex quickly, didn't we?" She flashed a grin at him. "Mr. Rigby, on the other hand, encountered a little snip of a girl who lay there like a sack of flour. He didn't much care for that, so he found his pleasures elsewhere."

Bill cleared his throat. "So he died and left you a young widow. Anyone after that?"

Eleanor let out a sigh. "I'm not going to lie to you, Will. I'd take a lover now and then, always discreetly and never for long. They knew I didn't love them. I knew they didn't love me. We were lonely."

Bill frowned. "Why didn't you just come back to Poplar Gap?"

"To whom? I managed to find out you'd gone off to Korea and married a woman from Humphrey when you got back. For all I knew, you were happy as a clam. I couldn't mess that up, don't you see?"

Bill patted her hands. "I understand. But we weren't married all that long. We had a son; she died of pneumonia in '62. After that, I mostly stayed on the mountain with Ethan, raising him, teaching him myself. Then he married a Cherokee woman." Bill smiled. "You'd have loved her, Nora. Her name was Walela. Hummingbird. Oh, she was a beauty, too."

"Was?"

Bill grimaced, the tears close again. "They lived in Humphrey and the baby came fast. Big, too. She was at home, and… she didn't make it. Took days to get word to me."

Chip interrupted. "This man has done a great job with Ian, Eleanor. College educated, handsome as a movie star. *Hard* worker. Really knows the mountain, too."

Eleanor smiled. "I can't wait to meet him. Where is he now?"

Bill and Chip exchanged glances. Bill looked at the clock on the mantel. "I'm hoping he's back from hunting by now, so he can, um, meet Tina."

Eleanor's eyes narrowed. "Tina is on the *mountain*? Is she all right?"

Chip turned his face away. "She was fine when we left her."

Eleanor was quick to pick up on the tension that suddenly filled the air. "You left… what have you done, Will?"

Bill stood up and began to pace around the room. "I thought I was dying, Nora. I wanted to find a good woman for

Ian. I've got all my affairs in order, and Chip said she was something wonderful—"

"She *is* something wonderful!" Eleanor was angry. She glared at Chip and pointed at him. "You! You caused that leak, didn't you? Of all the hare-brained ideas, I wonder why she didn't just call me? I could have found somebody—"

Sheepishly, Chip pulled Tina's phone out of his pocket and gave it a little wave.

"Well, I swanny. I know I haven't seen you in a lifetime, Will Cameron, but I never thought you'd go and do something like this."

"She's safe, Nora. I promise you. Ian'll take care of her. She's safe with him."

Eleanor arched an eyebrow. "Well, until I know that, you two aren't going anywhere. I'll be damned if I'm letting you out of my sight until that precious girl is standing in front of me, so you can just bed down here for the night."

Bill sat back on the couch, squirming a little. He gave a nervous cough. "She, well, she's not that precious. Told me, herself, she isn't pure. I wanted someone better for Ian."

Eleanor stood, her hands on her hips. "Not precious? Not as precious as bedding a fifteen-year-old in a hay loft? Or taking a wife you didn't love? Or me spreading my legs for an old goat to save my Daddy's store? Not as precious as crying myself to sleep all those nights after some man I didn't even know left me 'cause I was worn out from missing you? Don't you dare talk to me about precious. If your precious Ian is half as good a person as Tina Edwards, I'll be surprised."

With that, Eleanor stormed down the hall to her bedroom and slammed the door. Chip looked at Bill. Bill looked at the door. "So," Chip said.

Bill walked to the window and closed the curtains. "Let's button up as best we can, bring in as much firewood as will fit, just in case this goes bad." He opened the door of the other bedroom and nodded. "Couch okay with you?"

Before Chip could answer, Eleanor opened her door a crack and called, "Will, would you come here a minute?"

Bill shrugged at Chip and ambled down the hall. The door closed on him. Chip waited. And waited. Finally, he got a drink of water from the kitchen and lay down on the bed in the spare room. *Looks like Mr. Bill won't be needing it after all.*

10

Ian Cameron

T*his is intolerable. I will press charges, I will write letters, I will scream to whoever will listen.* Aloud, Tina yelled, "This aggression will not stand!" It was a favorite line from an old comedy, *The Big Lebowski*, but there was nothing funny about her situation. Her arms hurt from being in a cramped position, her legs hurt from the unexpected hike earlier, and she really needed to pee. That mug of tea was doing a number on her.

She wondered how long it would take for the fire to die out. Maybe a bear had mauled Ian. Maybe Bill and Chip as well! Maybe the very bear they'd seen earlier. Maybe Chip's truck would crash, and no one would know where she was, and she would die of dehydration and hunger. Her mind told her she was being melodramatic, but dammit, she was tied up on top of a mountain with some Neanderthal Scotsman headed her way. If he ever showed up. At the moment, Tina wasn't sure which scenario was preferable.

The loneliness and shock of it all sent her thoughts back to the frat party. Waking up alone on the lounge chair, bloodied and bruised—she had to admit that that morning was worse than this. She was warm and dry and could see that the kitchen had food. Inside the old refrigerator, there was probably water or juice. If she could get out of the chair, she'd find a bathroom and nourishment and she would get the hell out of Dodge. *Oh, God, what if they have an outhouse? No, Chip mentioned a septic tank. Whew.*

Even sitting by the fireplace, Tina sensed that the temperature outside had dropped. The sun was setting. She'd been sitting there for hours, she speculated. Her shoulders ached. She made little circles with her feet. She counted the number of logs for one wall. She studied the room. No books in sight, which didn't bode well for the Cameron intellect. No television or radio. "Alexa, play Diana Krall!" she announced loudly in a deep voice, passing the time, a stab at humor.

To her surprise, she saw a flicker of light in one corner of the kitchen as the opening chords to *Peel Me A Grape* were heard. "Well, I'll be damned," Tina muttered. *At least there'll be a soundtrack to my imminent demise.* She was torn. She should work at getting loose, but then what? Chip had known where all the traps were in the woods. She had no clue if he was telling the truth or just trying to scare her. Everything he'd said and done had been a kind of lie, hadn't it? Even if she'd paid closer attention to their circuitous route, though, it was dark. Something must have happened to Chip and Cameron. To Ian. She heard a light fluttering noise on the tin roof. *Is it raining?*

In answer, the front door swung open and a man, unidentifiable in hat, coat and scarf, burst inside with a sigh. Snowflakes dusted his profile, and as he stood there, immobile by the sight before him, little puddles of fallen and melted flakes dotting the floor around him. He carried a gun in one hand and in the other, what appeared to be *rabbits?* Ian Cameron stared at Tina. Tina stared back. Diana Krall ended the song.

Peel. Me. A. Grape. Sloowwly.

Just as slowly, Ian laid the rabbits down and put the gun on its hooks over the door. He took off the layers of clothing until he stood there, frowning, in a younger version of his grandfather, but also very different. He was tall and slender, with broad shoulders that hinted at pure muscle underneath his bright red flannel shirt. Tina guessed that his jeans must be lined with flannel for warmth, too, because they seemed heavier than normal.

Ian's thick black hair was to his shoulders. His skin was ruddy, slightly weather-beaten. His face was smooth. It was his eyes that commanded attention, the clearest blue that Tina had ever seen, and she realized her jaw had dropped. He was absolutely the handsomest creature she had every laid eyes on.

Suddenly, she shook herself. "Your grandfather tied me up so I wouldn't leave," she said hoarsely. "And I really need to pee."

Ian laughed. "My grandfather did *what*? He must have had a good reason." Eyes twinkling, he slowly picked up the rabbits and took them to the sink, where he began dressing them. "Too cold to do this outside, sorry," he said. "I didn't catch your name."

"Kristina Edwards, Tina, your grandfather's tenant and captive. Please, mister. Is there a bathroom in this godforsaken place?"

Ian stopped what he was doing to frown at her. "God hasn't forsaken this place, Miss Edwards. And I haven't forsaken my manners, either. I apologize. I forgot about your other predicament."

Wiping his hands on a towel, Ian walked over and quickly untied the knot. "You could've gotten out of this easily if you'd tried harder," he said. "It's just a bowline. Bathroom's the first door by the stairs."

Tina rubbed her hands and arms to get circulation flowing again. "Well, excuse me. If I'd known it was a *bowline*, I would've been gone when you got here," she snapped, walking stiffly to the bathroom door.

Inside, she found a little cabinet with a sink, a toilet with a wooden lid, and a metal washtub that had been converted to accommodate plumbing pipes. *Of course, the seat is up,* she thought. It was an odd thought. She was probably the first woman to be inside the cabin in decades. It sent a shiver up and down her spine as she relieved herself. *Thank God for simple pleasures. I could just stay in here, lock myself in. I'd be okay for a few days with just water.* But when she glanced up at the door, she saw that there was no lock. *Figures.*

Tina decided that as soon as Ian was distracted sufficiently, she would grab her coat and run. She had made the mistake of trusting Chip, but this man, she knew nothing about. And what she knew about men was not positive. She couldn't depend on Chip coming back for her, certainly. Maybe they ran a sex trafficking ring, lured young women up here, had their way with them, then sold them to the highest bidder. *Nah. Bill Cameron's just a nut.*

Tina looked at her reflection in the little mirror above the sink and rolled her eyes. She'd braided her hair and wrapped it around her head, Amish mode, but her knit hat had messed it up considerably. The tromp through the woods had dirtied her face, and angry tears had left streaks. Ian probably thought she was a poacher or trespasser his grandfather had caught and tied up until the authorities arrived. *Authorities.* Would anyone be looking for her yet? Was Eleanor concerned?

Tina washed her face and dried it with the towel hanging from a hook, feeling much better. When she came out, Ian was still working in the kitchen, glancing now and then out the window. "It's really coming down now," he said.

Tina edged closer to her coat and tried to sound nonchalant. "I wonder what could be keeping your grandfather and Chip?"

In answer, Ian pointed a bloody finger at the window and went back to skinning the animals he had shot. "Not your optimum travel weather." He sounded cheerful enough. "Fried rabbit, coming up. I'll fix enough for them too, but I doubt they'll be here, not with it coming down like that. Not for a few hours, anyway." He stopped working to look at her but got no response.. "We don't have to talk if you don't want to. I'm used to the quiet."

Tina stood near the door, watching Ian carefully. When he stooped low to get a pan from a cabinet, Tina silently unhooked her coat from the peg and turned the doorknob. The air was freezing. She gasped, hurriedly put the coat on and sprinted across the clearing. The snow was now falling so fast and thick that she had trouble seeing the opening she had come through with Chip. There was no light other than what the cabin gave off. She stood at the edge of the trees for a moment, deciding in which direction to head, then ventured blindly into the woods.

Seconds later, Ian shouted above the wind just a few feet behind her, "Stop!" In one motion, he picked her up, fireman style, and threw her over his shoulder, carrying her back across the little clearing. Tina pounded on his back and tried to thrash about, but he ignored her attempts to free herself as his long legs strode purposefully to the cabin.

Inside, Ian pulled a key from his pocket and locked the cabin door from the inside.

Great, Tina thought. *Now I'm really a prisoner.*

Without a word, he carried her to the other door at the end of the cabin and yanked it open with fury. He put her down roughly and pulled off her coat. Pushing her down on the bed, he took off his own coat and threw it onto the floor.

Tina's eyes darted around the room in search of a weapon, a candlestick, a book, anything she could grab and throw at this madman. In horror, she bolted upright at what she saw instead. Ian unbuckled his belt and pulled it from the waistband of his jeans. *He's going to rape me.* She had no knowledge of the rape at college, but every fiber of her being was on alert now. Instead of unzipping his jeans, however, she watched him loop the leather strap until he had a weapon of his own.

He sat down on the bed, roughly dragging her body down across his lap. "When I say stop, you *stop*!" Ian reared back his hand and brought the belt down on Tina's bottom. Even through her jeans, the blow smarted.

Tina couldn't believe what was happening, as she writhed with all her might to get away. "You're *spanking* me? Are you kidding? *Ow!* You're hurting me! Ow!"

Smack! Smack! Smack! On and on, it went, until tears were streaming down Tina's face. It was humiliating. And frightening. What kind of man was this?

Breathing heavily, Ian stopped striking her. Tina held her breath and made her body go limp, hoping the ordeal was over. She made a slight move.

"Oh, no, you don't," Ian said, holding her down more firmly. "I'm not through with you yet. You have no idea how serious this is. In fact—" With his left hand still pinning her to his knees, Ian laid his belt on the bed and reached around to unbutton Tina's jeans. He pulled them back, exposing the soft white flesh of her buttocks. There were faint red stripes where the belt had irritated her skin.

"Please don't rape me," she moaned. "Please!

Ian drew in a sharp breath and blew it out slowly. "I need to make sure you remember this. We've got a long night ahead of us." Picking up the belt again, he struck her again.

If Tina had thought she was in pain before, this changed her perspective. *Smack! Smack! Smack! Smack!* A final blow, and her cry was one of momentary agony. This time when she went limp, it was genuine. *He's won. I couldn't fight back now if I tried. This is when he pushes me back onto the bed, or maybe the floor?*

He'll have his way with me, and I will never recover. I'll have to leave. She had a rush of panic. What if he *never* let her leave? What had Chip gotten her into?

Ian maneuvered her onto the bed and, oddly, turned his back on her. "You can rest here until supper's ready," he said. He walked out and closed the door behind him.

Tina winced as she touched her bottom, then she pulled her jeans and panties back up. Curling up in a little ball on the bed in the small, dark room, she sobbed, even more afraid and confused now and so very tired. She lay back on the soft pillow and pulled a blanket up over herself from where it had been folded neatly at the foot of the bed. She looked out the window. There were no stars, no moon, just swirling snowflakes. She'd never seen snow before, and it was beautiful. Swirling. Twirling. She closed her eyes and was back on the dance floor in Richard's arms, twirling around and around. As he bent his head down to kiss her, she drifted off to sleep.

It felt like only a moment had passed when the light of the other room silhouetted Ian in the doorway. "The food's ready. You can come eat if you want. Or sleep. Up to you."

Tina lay there, wondering what to do. She had no desire to be in the same room with him, but she hadn't eaten anything all day, wanting an early start. Delicious new smells wafted her way from the next room. Wincing, she managed to get up, throwing the blanket aside.

When she walked stiffly into the room, Ian stood up from the table. Unexpectedly, he pulled a chair out for her at the table, which he had set sparingly but with all the essentials. There were red checked napkins, tin plates, utensils, even a bottle of ketchup. He'd fried the rabbit in flour, and there were also canned green beans, spiced apple slices, and hot biscuits and butter that had been shaped into a pretty round mold. There was water to drink. She waited while he bowed his head for a silent prayer, she guessed, and ate only when he did.

Anything might set someone like this off. She'd have to be more careful.

Ian buttered a biscuit for himself, then buttered another and handed it across to her.

"Thank you," she said softly. "Everything tastes good. I've never had rabbit before."

Ian said nothing but nodded. They ate in silence, Tina acutely aware of every chewing noise she made, every swallow. The fire was no longer roaring, and she shivered slightly. Without a word, Ian scooted his chair back and put a few more logs on the fire before sitting back down and resuming his meal.

Ian would not let her help clear the table or wash the dishes. "I can put music on if you want," he said, but she shook her head. The quiet was fine, with the pop of the wood burning. Tina had resigned herself to spending the night in the cabin with this stranger, but she was prepared to fight him tooth and nail if he tried anything. Anything *else*. Her bottom still stung.

When his work was finished, Ian sat in the upholstered rocking chair with a deep frown. His hair shone in the firelight as Tina reminded herself that she did not like men, least of all this one.

They sat in silence for several minutes until Tina found her voice. "Why did you do that?"

"Do what?"

"Spank me like a child and then pull my chair out for me. And why the belt? Why not just spank me with your hand?" Growing up, she and Layla had rarely gotten into trouble, but their grandmother had swatted their bottoms with her hand. The belt had made it seem even more barbaric. "It seems incongruous, contradictory."

The edges of Ian's mouth turned up ever so slightly. "I am aware of the definition of incongruous. I spanked you like a child because you behaved like a child. It was for your own good. I have a feeling my grandfather tied you up more for your safety than anything else. And when I told you to stop, you resisted. If you'd taken one more step, a bear trap would have taken off your foot. He paused. "I used a belt because that's the way I was disciplined. My grandfather always said that the touch of his hand was for love. The belt was to teach me."

His hand is for love. She suddenly realized that even as he had handled her roughly, there had been a sense of something else. Even when she was afraid he would rape her, she knew deep down that he would not be violent with her. Tina felt a pang at the end of her spine, imagining the shock of sharp metal teeth biting into her flesh. Chip had been careful to keep her safe on the way there, but she'd only half believed his story of traps. "So Chip's tale of traps was true?"

Ian nodded gravely. "You have no idea how much my grandfather values his privacy. Until you, Chip and my parents were the only people he's allowed up here since the company put in the electricity and plumbing. And that's been before I was born."

"You've lived here alone with him after they, after your mother died?"

Ian nodded again. "She died in childbirth. If she'd been at a hospital, of course, or maybe even had a midwife… anyway, that's what happened."

"My parents died when I was young. She died here? And your father?"

Firelight etched the grimace on Ian's face. "Her death broke him utterly." He looked at Tina sadly. "But no, they lived in Humphrey, in one of my grandfather's rental houses. I came fast, and I was big. There was no time." He sighed, as if it had been his fault. "She was full-blooded Cherokee, beautiful. I've got pictures up in my room to prove it. Anyway, my father started drinking heavily. One night, he left me with someone then wrapped his truck around a power pole. It took a while to get word up to my grandfather, but when he heard, he came down and got me."

Tina was fascinated, in spite of herself. "You've lived up here all that time?"

Ian shook his head, and Tina saw the Native American influence in the very way he carried himself. "I went to a Cherokee boarding school, graduated from UNC. I always called the mountain home, though. It's the only place I've ever considered living full-time."

So much for my no book theory. "Your grandfather," she began cautiously.

"Yes. He gets odd ideas from time to time. And he's usually right."

Tina stared at the fire. "Do you know why I'm here?"

Ian smiled, more relaxed than he had been. "Why do *you* think you're here?"

The anger returned like a flood. "Your grandfather hatched some ridiculous plan with Chip to get me up here and become your—"

"My—"

Tina blushed. "He thinks he's dying and wants you to have a companion before he goes and I was supposed to be her, but I'm not good enough," she blurted out in one breath.

In response, Ian made a low sound but said nothing, just rocked slowly back and forth, his strong hands entwined on his stomach. "My grandfather thinks he's dying. I do not agree. The idea that I should have a companion is not altogether unpleasant, but I can assure you, I am capable of finding a woman without kidnapping one."

Tina let out a breath. *I'll just bet you are.* "It wasn't really kidnapping, I suppose. My car ran out of gas, and Chip brought me up here before," her jaw dropped, "he *planned* it! He knew I'd run out of gas and was waiting! He must have done something to the car; *that's* why the door wasn't closed all the way." Her eyes narrowed. "But it was your grandfather's idea. Chip spied on me, befriended me, gained my complete confidence." Without realizing it, she had begun to cry.

Ian made no move to comfort her. How could he? He'd spanked her soundly just an hour earlier. She was stuck in the home of a man who'd tied her up. "I'm sorry this has happened," he said calmly, "but it's not the end of the world. You're safe, I assure you. Tomorrow morning, I'm sure they'll be back, and we'll get it straightened out. You can sleep in Grandfather's room where I sp—"

"What makes you think I won't try to leave again?"

Something like disappointment flashed in Ian's clear blue eyes, obviously a genetic contribution from his paternal side. "I think you're smarter than that. I've *never* seen it snow this hard, for this long. It's bitterly cold out there, and you'd be hours from shelter. There are still bears not in hibernation. There are traps everywhere. An electric fence. Surely, one night under the same roof with me is not worth the risk." A statement, not a question.

"Is there a lock on the bedroom door?"

Ian covered a smile by coughing into his hand. "There's a chair in the corner you can wedge under the doorknob, but you have no need to worry about your virtue."

"Thanks for the tip. The chair method it is, then. My *virtue*," she added bitterly as she walked to the bedroom, "wasn't good enough for your grandfather, either."

11

Concerns from Afar

K eith Henderson had his feet up in the recliner as Layla walked by, headed to the kitchen. "Is Angela down for the night?" he asked.

"Finally." Layla came in a moment later, carrying a glass of wine. "I'm so glad she's sleeping through the night now. I can indulge myself with a nightcap." She sat down on the couch, stretching her neck from side to side as she tucked her feet under her. "What?"

Keith smiled. "You're just so pretty. I enjoy looking at you."

Layla snorted and took a dainty sip of Chardonnay. "So I don't need to worry about you running off with any younger teachers?"

Keith shook his head. "Not a bit. Now the teacher's *aides* might be an issue. Some of them are *totally* hot." He caught the pillow Layla threw at him.

"What did Kristina have to say tonight? Think Chip will pop the question to Francine?" Every night, Layla either called her sister or received a call. He enjoyed the descriptions of her life in the mountains and was particularly grateful for Chip. He sounded like a great guy. And of course, being a teacher himself, he loved hearing about her classes. He was glad the sisters were close again. For a while, it had been rough.

"I thought maybe she had called while I was nursing Angela. I haven't heard from her. I guess I could call her now." She took a sip. "Mm, that's good. I never realized how much energy goes into taking care of a baby." Layla picked up her cell phone from the end table, punched her sister's speed dial, waited and put it back down. "Voicemail. Odd. Do you think everything's okay? Should I be worried?"

Keith shook his head. "She's doing great now. Maybe she's already in bed. You can try her again in the morning." He slid the pillow under his shirt. "Now be honest. When your belly looked like this, did I show you enough attention?"

Layla made kiss lips at her husband. "You were amazing, honey. Remember how you used to tell me to turn so you could see my profile? I never *once* felt unappreciated."

"Or unwanted." Keith pulled the pillow out and threw it back to the couch. He pulled the side lever to make the chair recline and reached out his arms. "Come here, you."

Setting her wine on an end table, Layla snuggled onto his lap. "I love you, you know."

Keith responded by hugging her more tightly. "You'd better. Those teacher's aides think I'm fucking *won*derful."

Layla chuckled. "Yeah, but do they put out? Speaking of which, let me doze here a minute, then you can have your way with me, I promise."

After a long day at school, and a long day with Angela, the two quickly fell asleep.

Worth was filling up his coffee cup in the hotel when he overheard the Weather Channel on the breakfast buffet area TV. Record snow in western North Carolina. He wondered briefly if Kristina's school had closed. *Tina. I have to remember to call her that now.*

With his magazine business dispensed with quickly, he hoped he could devote today to redemption. Or justice. He'd located two Richard Barrows, one a law student at a city an hour away, one a golf pro locally. He'd check him out first. Maybe he wouldn't have to rent a car and make the drive. *Fingers crossed.*

The concierge had arranged for a taxi to pick him up in five minutes. *Better head outside.* Leaving his cup on the counter with a generous tip underneath for the hotel staff, he waved to the front desk staff and exited the revolving door. It was a beautiful day, sunny and warm, several time zones away from the cold back east. And that record snow. *I'll bet it's beautiful, though.*

Meadowlark Country Club was as posh as they came. He just hoped it wasn't a wild goose chase. "I may be right back out," he told the driver. "Would you wait ten minutes in case? Otherwise, I'll be here a while. I'll settle up with the hotel, if that's okay with you."

Soon he was out of the dry heat and into air conditioning. It was hard to imagine it was winter at all. *I guess that's why so many people retire here.* His mother had houses scattered around the country. He'd have to tell her about this part of Arizona.

"May I help you, sir?" A handsome, muscled young man in a tennis outfit had seen him looking around the lobby. His nametag read "Kyle."

"Thank you, Kyle. I'm looking for Richard Barrows. Is the pro shop open yet?"

Disappointment registered briefly on Kyle's face. *Lucky Richard,* he thought, *although I thought he played for the other team.* "He's there. I'll be glad to take you." *Oh* boy, *would I be glad. That shaved head, the beard. Be still my heart.*

"Lead the way. And thanks." It was both Worth's natural curiosity and his background in journalism that prompted him to ask people about their lives. Usually, he walked away from encounters knowing many details about whomever he'd spoken with, realizing that they'd discovered very little about him. From his observation, people weren't all that interested in other people, but they sure did love to talk about themselves.

By the time Kyle and Worth arrived at the pro shop, Worth knew how long Kyle had been a tennis instructor—five years— and that a recent break-up with his first steady boyfriend had been devastating. His father was a jeweler, and his mother worked alongside him. They'd been married forty years. "That's the key to a lasting relationship, my dad always says. Do everything together. He takes her shopping, on business trips."

"My wife works with me too," Worth said as they walked.

Instead of asking about it, Kyle moved on to the weather and its effect on the curliness of his hair, proving Worth's observation once again.

"Here we are," Kyle said breezily, opening the glass door for Worth.

Worth glanced at his watch. The taxi driver might still be there if this wasn't his guy. *But maybe he is.*

A handsome, tanned man waved from behind the counter. "Be right with you, just finishing something up. Hey, Kyle. How's it hangin'?"

Kyle blushed and excused himself with a grunt of a good-bye. "Lesson in five, gotta run."

As the man jotted a few notes on a pad, Worth watched him. The age was right. "Richard Barrows?"

The man gave a little flourish with his hand. "At your service. What can I do you for? Are you joining the club?"

Worth absently checked the price of a pair of golf pants. "No, I wanted to ask you about a personal matter."

Richard Barrows frowned. "Look, I don't know what Kyle led you to believe, but I'm not interested in—"

Worth smiled at him. "Women?"

Richard frowned again, confused. "I *am* interested in women. I thought—"

"I'm inquiring on behalf of a particular woman you might have been interested in several years ago. Or at least knew. Any information you have would be appreciated. *Greatly* appreciated."

A look crossed Richard's face, indicating that perhaps money would be involved. He walked around the counter and over to Worth. "I know a lot of women, Mr.—"

"Vincent. Dillingsworth Vincent." Worth pulled a card from his pocket and handed it to Richard. "My wife's sister-in-law is the woman I'm inquiring about. Kristina Edwards. Ever heard of her?"

Richard's tan face suddenly paled. Worth could see the wheels turning in his mind. *Should I tell the truth, or should I lie?* "Kris—yes," he said slowly. "She went to the same college I did. We graduated the same year."

Worth's expression did not change. "Great. Is there a place we could sit down and chat a few minutes?"

Richard glanced around the store, hoping someone would interrupt them. "There are some chairs over here." He led Worth to a little waiting area for impatient husbands to read the latest golf magazine while their wives shopped. The men sat down. Worth said nothing.

Richard looked at his watch. "Listen, I don't want to be rude, but I'm on the clock."

Worth smiled. "If you need to help a customer, I can wait." He looked around. "Fortunately, it's just the two of us at present."

"Right." Richard was obviously uncomfortable.

"Right."

Richard waited a few seconds. "So, why the interest in Kristina?"

Worth leaned in slightly. "Kristina went to a frat party her senior year, Richard. Something happened to her there. Something bad. I want to find the person, or persons, who are responsible."

"What, uh, what happened to her?"

Worth couldn't be sure why Richard Barrows was squirming, but he certainly looked guilty. "I can't go into the details." *Which is true, because I don't know them.* "But a few months after the incident, Kristina received a sizable grant. One that she hadn't applied for. Do you know anything about the Exagorà Foundation?"

Richard coughed. "Ah, the—"

"Everett Barrows is one of the foundation's trustees. Isn't he your father?"

Oddly, Richard looked out the window. "Well, my father is on the board of lots of—"

"Richard, cut the bullshit." Worth's eyes followed Richard's gaze. Three men in a golf cart were heading for the green. They had put on both weight and age, but they were still recognizable.

Instead, Richard stood. If they had been in a police interrogation room, this would have been where the accused "lawyered up." Worth could see it on his face. The conversation was over. *But I'm not through with you yet.* "Okay, Richard,"

Worth said quietly. "We can do this another way. I'll be in touch."

Worth did not look back as he walked calmly from the pro shop. He headed straight for the tennis courts he and Kyle had passed on the way, where Kyle and his tennis student were taking a water break. "Kyle!" he called from behind the chain link fence along the sidewalk.

Kyle trotted over to the fence with a big smile. "Hey! What's up?"

Worth held up a $100 bill. "Can you think of anyone who might help me catch up with a threesome?"

Kyle laughed. "Honey, I can think of a whole list of folks who'd enjoy a threesome with you. Just name the place and time."

Worth looked at his feet. "Let me rephrase that." He made a little face at Kyle. "There are three men who just headed out to play golf. I'd like to find them."

Kyle shrugged and grinned. "Can't blame a boy for trying. Our lesson's over. I can take you."

It took longer than Worth had hoped for Kyle to explain to a staff member the situation and check out a club cart, but soon they were heading for the trio of men. They passed several groups of golfers enjoying the day, but it wasn't long before Worth said, "Slow down. This is them just ahead."

"Do you want me to wait for you?" Kyle checked his watch. "I don't have another lesson for another hour."

"That would be great, Kyle. Thanks."

"Easiest hundred I ever made, boss. I aim to please." Kyle's grin was a leer, and by now, the two were getting along well enough that Worth just laughed. Not his cup of tea, but flattering at some level.

Worth waited until one of the men made his shot before he approached the group. "Excuse me," he said. Three men in their late forties or early fifties, he guessed, turned around in unison. From their clothing, jewelry and clubs, he could tell that the men were wealthy.

Worth reached into his pocket and handed each man one of his cards. "Dillingsworth Vincent, gentlemen."

One of the men nodded as he read the card. "Magazine, eh? Which one of us did you want to interview first?" Apparently, he was used to being sought after.

Worth smiled. "I'm interested in the Exagorà Foundation."

The men exchanged sideways looks. "I think you were given faulty information, Mr. Vincent. The Exagorà Foundation has been dissolved, as of… what was it, Everett? A year, year and a half ago?"

Everett Barrows nodded and narrowed his eyes at Worth. "That's right. We formed a foundation but then changed our minds about it. Dissolved it completely."

"Huh," Worth said. "Well then, please excuse the interruption, gentlemen. I'll be on my way." As he walked back to the golf cart, he called over his shoulder, "I'll let Miss Edwards know to proceed in another direction."

Everett Barrows held up a hand to stop him and caught up to him. "What do you mean 'proceed'?"

He didn't even pretend not to know a Miss Edwards. "Everett Barrows. And Todd Bailey, Senior? Clarence O'Day?"

The other men stepped forward. O'Day was working up an attitude. "Now see here, Vincent. You can't just spring something like this on us out of nowhere. We demand to know what Miss Edwards has told you, and what her plans are!"

Worth exchanged a glance with Kyle, who was clearly amused by the whole situation. *All right, going out on a limb here.* "How about I tell you a story instead? It's about three college boys with absolutely everything going for them who drugged an innocent young woman, raped her, beat her half to death, then cried to their daddies to fix things."

Bailey sputtered, "They did *not* beat her!"

"Shut up, Todd," Clarence snarled.

Bailey was indignant. "My boy isn't the one who drugged her, you know. They talked him into it."

Everett was suddenly contrite. "Look, Vincent. Theoretically, let's say the story sounds vaguely familiar. And that, theoretically, the boys know what they did was wrong. Theoretically. That a drug was given to Miss Edwards without her knowledge." He looked close to tears and studied something far in the distance. "You think you've raised your son right, and," he looked back at Worth, "what can we do to fix this? To end it, once and for all?" The other men clustered around him.

O'Day's tone changed as well. "W-we thought she might press charges. We were getting prepared for that particular nightmare, but she never did. We were so thankful, we thought maybe if we helped her out financially, it would…" His voice trailed away.

"Redeem your sons?"

The three men stood in the sun, arms crossed, suddenly looking small and weak. It was not something they were used to.

Worth bit his lip, thinking what to do next. "Gentlemen, the money you gave Miss Edwards *did* help. She had a very rough time of it, as perhaps you can imagine. Or perhaps not. She'd lost her parents as a child. She lost her virginity to whichever one of your asshole sons got to her first. Her reputation was damaged on campus. She questioned her own actions. She lost her confidence. She graduated and got a job, but she was a mess. Almost losing her sister last Christmas apparently pushed her over the edge, I can't really say. But she finally sought therapy and made some dramatic life changes. That young woman's strength and perseverance redeemed her life. Your money did help, gentlemen," Worth said, "but it did not redeem your sons. It will *never* redeem your sons."

Everett Barrows stepped closer to Worth. "Does Miss

Edwards need anything? Anything at all? The, um, foundation could be revived, don't you think?" He turned with a look of pleading to his companions. Each man murmured more-or-less enthusiastic assent.

Worth sighed. "The statute of limitations has run out. I checked. This isn't the most victim-friendly state, by any means."

Relief washed over the men's faces, but to their credit, they had the sense to be embarrassed. "Forgive us," O'Day murmured. "They are still our sons."

Worth nodded. "I understand. And I understand what living with a past can do to a person." He stepped close enough to the three men that they could feel his breath as he continued. "But you'd better believe that if it were still possible, I would match you penny for penny, million for million, to put those useless sons of yours away for the rest of their lives, or whatever a jury would give them."

He almost felt sorry for the men. Almost. "The only person who can forgive you, however—and certainly the only person who can forgive your sons—is teaching autistic kids in the mountains of North Carolina."

12

Snowed In

Once during the night, Tina quietly removed the chair from under the knob of the bedroom door and tiptoed to the bathroom. The fire had died to embers in the fireplace, but she realized that even fully dressed, the room was surprisingly cold. Surely, the Camerons had some sort of back-up heat that cut on when it got this chilly. *I can see my breath, for heaven's sake.* When she closed the bathroom door and flicked on the light switch, she immediately discovered the reason for the plunging temperature. No electricity. If they *did* have a back-up, it was of no use now.

Tina sat down to relieve herself and wondered if she should flush. Because she was ignorant of the plumbing details of the mighty Cameron clan, she decided against it. She allowed herself a quick turn of the faucet to rinse her hands, but nothing came out. *I'd really like a toothbrush*, she thought and went back to bed.

She had closed the curtains, but there was no moonlight tonight. The room was pitch black. She listened for sounds. The embers in the fireplace sang quietly, punctuated by an occasional pop. She thought it must still be snowing outside, although perhaps not as heavily. She could hear the sound of her breath, which brought to mind her high school literature class' study of Edgar Allan Poe's *The Telltale Heart*.

My heart is half-frozen—no sound there. She thought about the man sleeping directly above her. They were separated only by a ceiling and floor. She heard a muffled sound, as if he had turned over in the bed and made the frame move a bit.

I'm in a house in a snowstorm with a man I don't know, no phone and now no electricity. At least I can probably leave in the morning, with or without Chip's truck. I'll talk Ian into walking me out of the woods— he seems decent enough if you overlook the spanking. I'll appeal to his honor. Noble savage and all that. She bit her lip. *Oh dear. That sounds as bad as Chip following Mr. Bill's orders and Francine's Confederate flag.*

Even with the blanket, she was cold. Tina felt around the dark room for the dresser and closet, hoping to find more bedding, but that was it. The trunk at the end of the bed? *Damn. Locked.* There was nothing to do but try to sleep. She vaguely remembered something she'd read with her mother when she was little. One of the *Little House* books by Laura Ingalls Wilder. There was a blizzard. If you went to sleep, you'd die. *Maybe I'm remembering it wrong.*

Tina let the tears flow, thinking of the happy years before the accident. Her father had been so tender, her mother so cheerful. She and Layla had never guessed it would all end so soon. *You can have that again,* a little voice spoke deep inside. *I have nothing to give a man. There's nothing left. They took it all.* For the first time in years, Tina cried herself to sleep.

When she woke again, she strained her ears. The snow had stopped. She practically shouted. This was good news! She had no idea how deep the snow on the ground would be, but probably just a few inches. It might ruin her boots—she'd never gotten around to using the weatherproofing Chip had given her—but that would be a small price to pay for getting the hell out of here. She'd have to find another place to live, of course. No way would she pay another cent to that mad man who had masqueraded as a reasonable landlord. Maybe Principal Clark would know of someone who could put her up temporarily.

Unbidden, a vision of Chip and Eleanor sitting around the table playing cards with her, laughing, sprang to her mind. She'd miss that. She'd miss *them*. Chip had been truly forlorn when he left her the day before. She groaned. It had only been about twelve hours, she guessed, since she'd been tied up. It felt like it had been days. Layla would be frantic. Eleanor, no, she'd have been reminiscing about high school with her old pal Will, laughing it up while she got spanked and force-fed fried rabbit.

The rabbit *had* been tasty, she had to admit. Tina reached behind her to touch the seat of her pants. Still tender, but better. She curled into a ball and drifted off to sleep again, tormented in her dreams by an enormous bear that made her drink poison and then tore out her heart. She saw his claws tear into her flesh, but she couldn't move. And she couldn't feel a thing.

Tina woke to a soft tap at the door. When she opened her eyes, faint sunlight streamed in around the heavy curtains, a crack here, a crack there. She got up, set the chair on the floor and opened the door.

"You're not going to believe this," Ian said grimly.

"I ran out of gas, was tied up, spanked, and ate a wild animal. I would believe anything," she said with a yawn, following him to the front door. When she tried to push it open, it didn't budge.

"Look out the window," Ian said.

Snow had blown in halfway up the side of the house. "We're trapped?"

"For the time being. If this was a regular snow, there'd be no problem, but this was no regular snow. It snowed hard, then the temperature dropped enough to freeze the stuff. It'll take a while."

Tina peered out the window at the bank of pure white. "If you break the window, I might be able to climb out onto the surface—

Ian stood with perfect posture, shaking his head. "I am not breaking the window, and you are not climbing out. This stuff would be treacherous."

Tina had an idea. "But the traps would be hidden, wouldn't they? I wouldn't need help getting to the road."

Ian chuckled as he closed the curtain back. "I'd rather keep the curtains open for light, but closed is better, to hold the heat in. Power's out, too."

"I know," Tina mumbled. She walked, slump-shouldered, to stand in front of the roaring fire Ian had going. Thoughtful. She could smell coffee, too. Was that bacon? Her mouth watered. "So what do we do now?"

"*We* eat our breakfast." Ian held a chair out for her, just as he'd done the night before, then brought over a platter of scrambled eggs and bacon. He'd cut open leftover biscuits and fried them in butter. There was hot coffee, honey, and cream. At the look in her eyes, he shrugged. "I know you're not supposed to open the refrigerator when the power goes off, but as cold as it was, I didn't see much risk. I got everything out and *then* started the fire."

"Good thinking," she mumbled through a bite of bacon, crispy, the way she liked it.

"Did you sleep well?"

"I made a few mistakes." Despite the circumstances, she laughed at the old joke her grandfather used to say. "I did. Thank you for asking. I was cold half the night. Had some bad dreams."

Ian sat back in his chair and drank his coffee. "What dreams? You know, we Native Americans have mad skills where dreams are concerned." His face was solemn, but his eyes twinkled.

Is he teasing me? What the hell. "The most vivid one," she said, not bothering to swallow before talking, "was a bear. It gave me poison to drink. Then it… it tore out my heart, only I couldn't feel it. I could see what it was doing, but I couldn't get away."

Ian nodded. "Dream bears can mean different things, but an aggressive bear reveals anger. Anger at someone else, anger at yourself." Tina made a face he couldn't fathom. "Or both?"

"Maybe."

"Anything else?" he probed. "What color was the bear?"

Tina rolled her eyes. "Seriously? It was a big bear, with big teeth and big claws, ripping my heart out. What does it fucking matter what color rug it would make?" *Tsk, tsk. Watch your language for the young Mr. Cameron. Grandpa wouldn't like that.*

Ian let out a breath. "You brought it up. Never mind." Quietly, he continued to eat.

The two sat eating and drinking without talking, for several minutes. *Patience was never my strong suit.* "The bear was brown. Not black, like the one Chip and I saw, or the one on your floor. Not a grizzly, but huge, overpowering. And definitely brown."

Something flickered in Ian's eyes, but he said nothing.

Tina laid down her fork. "What?"

Ian cleared his throat. "A brown bear could speak of brutal passions." He grunted. "But what do I know? If we had WiFi, we could look it up on my phone. Since yours is gone, I gather."

"The WiFi is out too? You had a *phone*, yesterday? You might have mentioned it." She pooched her lower lip out in mock pout. "So no Alexa, either?"

Ian chuckled. "That's right. You'd managed to find Alexa when I got here. Diana Krall, if I remember correctly."

Tina was impressed. "I love her voice. Deep, sexy." She shook her head to focus. "Breakfast is delicious, thank you. You're quite the paradox, Ian Cameron."

"How so?"

"You hunt wild rabbits and know how to cook them. You wore me out with the only spanking I've received since I was six, but then you held the chair for me. You live up here like a hermit, but you're college educated. You're Native American, but you have those beau… you have blue eyes." She stopped. "Oh, and you seem to be fairly normal despite being raised by a lunatic."

Ian's laugh was deep. And sexy. "I will let you in on a little secret. My grandfather is the smartest man I know. There's a lot of pain inside him, but he's no lunatic."

"Yeah, well, he's *something.*"

"Why did you get a spanking when you were six?"

Does he miss nothing? "If you must know, I was angry and poked a hole in my grandparents' screen door." She smiled, remembering. "And I had to help Grandpa repair it."

Ian nodded with approval—*as if I need it,* she thought—but frowned as he stood and carried his empty plate to the sink. "We'll just scrape the plates and wipe them a little. I think the pipes are frozen. Maybe just one or two, but we need to conserve water anyway, in case."

Tina took her plate over, waving her coffee mug as she talked. "In case what? Chip will be on his way, won't he? He always carries tools. Can't he just shovel his way inside?"

Ian's face was full of compassion. This was a city girl, after all. And this was a harsh introduction to the mountains. Harsh, even for him. "If Chip was able to get here, I think he'd be here already. My grandfather hasn't spent a night away from home in probably thirty years, maybe more. We don't know what happened to them, but *something* happened. They're not coming, Kristina. Not today."

Tina was startled at his use of her given name until she remembered she'd blurted it out when they met. "I go by Tina."

"I think Kristina suits you better," he said quietly.

Shrugging, Tina sat down on the bear rug in front of the fire. "Crisscross applesauce," she said sadly.

"Excuse me?"

She pointed to her legs without looking his way. "Crisscross applesauce. That's what we tell our students when we want them to sit on the rug for reading time. Maybe you'd prefer Indian style?" *Good grief. Go out of your way to push his buttons, why don't you?*

But Ian just smiled a half-smile. "You're a teacher. I guess I didn't ask yesterday. What grade?"

Tina shook her head, still staring at the flames. "All of the above. I work with students who are autistic. Sometimes they stay in school past graduation, even, if their parents don't think they're ready." She turned her head toward him. "But mostly younger. They're really something."

Ian sat down in the upholstered rocker. "So then. What to do. We could read by oil lamps or play cards, I suppose. There's chess, checkers, Scrabble."

"What was it like going to the Cherokee school?" The outstanding breakfast and coffee had gone a long way toward improving Tina's mood, even with the disappointing specula- tion concerning Chip. She kept putting her foot in her mouth, but she was genuinely interested in Ian's answer.

"Great! Also lonely. I missed being with my grandfather, but I loved school. And I learned about my heritage." Suddenly, he threw his head back. "I'll have to check the calen- dar, but I think we just passed one of the big celebration days. It completely slipped my mind." He made hand gestures in the air, as if he were making notes. "The moon should be almost at the quarter now, so yes. The New Moon ceremony would have been about, oh, eight days ago."

Tina turned toward him and hugged her knees close. "What do they do for that, I mean, *you*?"

"Cherokee tradition says that the world was created in the fall. The New Moon celebration was sort of the New Year. There was dancing, going to water. A priest would make predictions, that kind of thing."

"Going to water?"

Ian nodded. "A cleansing ritual. Water is sacred to the Cherokee. There are purifications for morning, at the new moon, after a battle. Water is clean, *was*. Kept clean by the traditions. The Cherokee didn't get sick like some did, way back when, because of that. At the New Moon Celebration, they would dip in the water seven times."

"I would *love* to dip in water right about now. I feel filthy. My clothes are dirty. My hair is dirty. *I'm* dirty."

"That can be remedied, if you can exercise some patience and a sense of adventure."

———

True to Ian's words, it had taken a lot of time and effort, but Tina was now submerged in a lovely bath. Using pots and buckets, they had heated gallons of water to boiling, poured it into the tub a bit at a time, and melted more snow until there was a sufficient amount in which to bathe. The water was neither hot enough to her taste nor too cold to tolerate. She didn't care. She was clean. She felt empowered. No power, no running water, but did that stop Kristina Edwards? *Hell no.*

Tina scrubbed every inch of her face, neck and body. It would almost be worth it to ask Ian to wash her back, but… *Don't be ridiculous.* She knew her hair was a mess, but she'd wash it last. Her eyes wandered around the little bathroom, stopping at the sight of a razor. She felt her legs. Practically a forest of stubble. Normally, she wouldn't care, but it was the New Moon ceremony recently, right? She thought, *this will be my symbolic cleansing. Maybe the water gods will look on me with favor.*

13

Friends Made

Ian knocked on the bathroom door just as Tina finished washing her hair. A shelf above the toilet held a mountain of towels, so she grabbed two. One for her hair, one for her... what would she wear? The thought of putting on the dirty clothes she'd been wearing around the clock was unpleasant, but what were the alternatives? The Cameron men's clothes would dwarf her.

"I, um, I don't have anything to put on," she stammered loudly.

"I'm way ahead of you," he said from the other side of the door. "May I open the door and hand you something?"

"No peeking," she warned.

The door opened a crack, and one hand emerged through it holding something white. "It's thin. Not warm enough. But when you're dressed, you can look for something else." Ian closed the door again.

He might have at least tried *to get a peek,* she thought crossly. *I suppose he doesn't look at me that way. I'm too, what? Too white? Too spoiled? Damaged goods?* This was, she realized, unfair. Ian knew nothing of her past and *would* know nothing of her past.

They'd tough it out for a day or so more, and then she'd be home.

The garment was obviously old and hand-sewn. No one wore such things these days. It was a woman's high-neck, long sleeved nightgown, several sizes too big, but at least she'd be covered. She had no idea what Ian meant about looking for anything else, but she was getting chilled and needed the fire.

As her bare feet padded across the chilly wood floor, Ian stood from the rocker and gestured for her to sit there. "I've got more hot water to add to the tub for myself. Be out in a bit." Tucking his clean clothes under one arm, he carried two buckets of steaming water from the kitchen and closed the door. Tina's eyes followed him all the way. *He's what, six-two? Three? Jet black hair, those eyes. Stop!*

Tina unwrapped her hair and draped both towels over chairs at the table. She finger-combed her long tresses as best she could. *Wherever Ian found this, maybe there are other things. A brush! Or not.* She was surprised he'd found the nightgown. There was not one thing in the cabin that revealed a woman had ever lived there. His grandmother, she recalled, had died years before his birth. *He never knew his mother,* she thought sadly. *At least we had a few years, Layla and I.* By now, her sister probably had the North Carolina State Police on speed dial.

Tina looked down, horrified. Her long, wet hair had rendered the bodice of the nightgown virtually transparent. "No, no, no, no, no," she murmured and stood in front of the fire, holding the fabric away from her body so the fire's heat could dry it. When the front was sufficiently opaque, she turned her back to the fire, playing with her hair so that it dried more quickly. *There's too much of it, that's all there is to it. Maybe I can get Ian to scalp me with his knife.* Her shoulders sank. *Again, with inappropriateness!* If she managed to leave without putting her foot in her mouth yet again, she'd be so grateful.

Tina reached behind her head and back and tested for

dampness, then she checked the nightgown's front again. *Dry enough that I don't flash him,* she thought wryly. *As if he would notice.* She turned around to face the fireplace again, leaning her hands on the mantle, glad of the sense of peace and warmth the crackling fire brought.

Lost in her thoughts, Tina neither heard the bathroom door open nor realized how long Ian stood transfixed when he stepped into the room.

Every curve of Tina's shapely silhouette was accented by the fire through the filmy nightgown. He was sure she had no idea how exposed she was. And he was *absolutely* sure she would not appreciate knowing—or seeing—how moved he was by the sight of her.

Despite the chill at that end of the house, he was suddenly very warm, embarrassed by the immediate physical response he had experienced. It had been a long time since he had seen a woman's body, and he didn't think he had ever seen one quite as lovely. Her hair hung below her waist, glowing in the firelight, but not a thick enough screen to hide her form completely.

"Rapunzel, Rapunzel, let down your hair," he said quietly as he walked to join her.

There was every reason in the world for Tina to despise this man, but everything he said and did—with the one exception —drew her to him. And even *that*, the spanking, she could halfway understand. She had been about to endanger herself, and he was frightened. *He was frightened for me. When has every happened, that a man thought more of me than himself?*

She turned to answer him with a little laugh. "Rapunzel. Is that an old Cherokee legend?" she teased, crossing her arms self-consciously. There was only one layer of fabric between him and her naked body. It was not an entirely unpleasant thought, just an unusual one.

Ian hung his damp towel over a chair the way she had done with hers and went into the kitchen. He poured something clear into two glasses and handed her one. "Little sips," he warned. "We'll keep all the doors closed, so the heat stays in this one area. I, um, I think we should both sleep out here. I'll keep the fire going through the night, but we don't have much dry firewood left. Tonight, we're good. Maybe tomorrow."

The liquid had a faint yeasty smell. She took a sip. It was definitely alcoholic, but the warming effect was delicious. "Where did you find the nightgown?" Tina asked, subconsciously pulling her hair in front, just in case he could see through the fabric.

Ian was having trouble looking her in the eye. He set his glass on the table. "Come with me, and I'll show you."

As Tina followed him to his grandfather's room, she couldn't help but notice the way his jeans hugged him. *He is all muscle, this one. What would it feel like to put my arms around him?* Ordinarily, she would dismiss such ideas immediately, but damn it, she'd been virtually kidnapped, tied up, spanked and nearly frozen. She deserved a few pleasant thoughts, didn't she? The irony of this did not escape her—a day or so ago, and she wouldn't have *had* pleasant thoughts about an attractive man.

Inside Bill Cameron's room, Ian told her to gather up all the bedding and pillows and take them to the living room. "I'll get the blankets upstairs, but here," he held up a little key, "I found this on the dresser, and it fits the trunk. My grandfather must have kept some of my grandmother's things."

He opened the trunk, and she knelt on the floor in front of it, careful to set her glass where it wouldn't turn over. Mrs.

Cameron had been a big woman, but the long underwear and woolen socks, the scarves and shawls, a wrap-around wool skirt, a sweater, she would make them work. "No time for fashion," she murmured. At the bottom of the trunk, she found a silver hairbrush and comb set, tarnished from years of storage. She held them up for Ian to see. "You're sure it's all right for me to use these?"

Ian made a little noise of approval. "My grandfather tied you to a chair, Kristina. I don't think it matters whether it is all right or not."

Tina put the clothes on the bed and pulled everything off together, knapsack style. Ian rolled up the mattress under one arm and carried two pillows under the other, to follow her into the living area.

They spread the mattress in front of the fire and Tina smoothed the sheet and blankets on top. While Ian headed upstairs for more bedding, she carefully folded the clothing on the table and wriggled her legs into the woolen stockings. Immediately, she felt warmer.

She was surprised when Ian returned with blankets only. She opened and closed her mouth a few times, unsure how to word her question.

"What is it?" Ian asked as he smoothed the additional blankets on top of the mattress. Tina frowned and bit her lower lip, pointing to the mattress. "Where, um, where are *you* going to sleep?"

"Kristina. I have on all my clothes. We'll be warmer together under all the covers this way, instead of dividing them up. Your virtue is safe, I can assure you."

That's what I'm afraid of, she thought ruefully. *Oh, stop it! He's a gentleman. He could have a girlfriend already, for all you know. You don't know him, and he doesn't know you.*

Tina snuggled under the mountain of blankets and watched as Ian added wood to the fire. Not wanting to lose him to sleep just yet, she asked what kind of wood it was. He squatted between the mattress and the fireplace, adding several thick logs. "These logs are oak. We cut ash and maple, too. Locust burns too hot. Pine and poplar aren't the best. Cedar, interestingly enough, is sacred to the Cherokee. You may have noticed some tall cedars as you came into the clearing. My mother planted them there as a gift to my grandfather."

Tina sat up on her side, leaning on her elbow. "I love the smell of cedar. My mother had a cedar chest from when she got married. My sister Layla has it now."

Ian sat down on the edge of the mattress, careful not to come into contact with the blankets hiding Tina's legs. Even so, it was difficult for him to concentrate. *It would be so easy, and so wrong.* "Perhaps tomorrow, the snow will have melted to the point that I can get out and check on things. If the water pipe froze under the house, that will be one thing. If it's closer to the well, that's better. And I can maybe dig out more firewood to dry. Who knows? Maybe we'll have cell service, and you can call Layla."

"And Chip. He owes me a drive to my house, I think."

Ian nodded. "I would agree with that."

"You don't own a vehicle?"

Ian looked at her with a grin. "Why would you think that?"

Tina frowned. "I guess because you haven't been in Poplar Gap for months? Chip drives your grandfather around?"

Ian smiled. "I've been away for several months. Otherwise, I might have known about my grandfather's little plan and stopped it before it started." He shook his head. "He is one stubborn old man. *Dying.* He will probably outlive us all."

Tina's eyes were on the fire, but every fiber of her being was aware of his nearness. "He was so intent on finding you a woman, a wife. Have you never brought a girlfriend to meet him?" *Were you away seeing someone? Inquiring minds want to know.*

Ian stared at the flames, glad for a distracting conversation. He was not prepared to get under the covers with this woman. Not just yet. "During college, I brought a few women home. Full of youthful enthusiasm, I thought anyone I liked would like the mountain, would like my grandfather." Almost in a whisper, he added, "Would love me for who I am."

Tina took another sip from her glass. "You've got to admit, it would take a special kind of woman to live up here all the time. But your car?"

"Truck. It's parked up the mountain a bit. There's another way in that's easier, less of a walk. I guess Chip wanted to go the long way, to quash any thoughts of heading out by yourself. Which did not quite work, as I recall." Ian picked up a slender branch and stirred the fire, shifting the logs to burn more efficiently.

Tina blushed. What would those hands feel like on her bare skin? The spanking had been painful, even through her jeans, but perhaps if he had touched her skin, he wouldn't have wanted to spank her as much as... I know, it was for my own good. But it still hurt. She frowned with a sudden thought. "You had a truck all the time? Why didn't you just take me home when you untied me?"

"You didn't ask." He grinned and gave a little shrug. "I suppose I was so taken with you from the first moment I saw you that I wanted to prolong your visit. Of course, I wasn't counting on Chip and Grandfather not returning soon. Or anticipating the snow of the century."

Tina smiled, obviously flattered. "You're right, I didn't ask.

It has been an adventure." She patted the spot next to her, a modest distance. "Coming to bed, dear?" she quipped.

Ian was not convinced yet that it would be safe for him to be under the covers with this beautiful woman. "Your dream. The brutal passions of the bear. He ripped your heart, but you didn't feel it. Did that remind you of anything? You didn't question my explanation."

Tina sat up on the mattress, cross-legged. She pulled the blanket up high on her lap. "I haven't been able to talk about this for a long time. I told my therapist. Not so long ago, I finally told my sister. I-I've come a long way, but I'm not the woman your grandfather had in mind for you, so it's all just as well."

Something flickered in Ian's eyes, but he said nothing.

Tina sighed and stared at the fire. "Oh, hell, what does it matter *who* knows at this point? It's not the first time a girl screwed up her life, and it won't be the last." Without looking at him, she told the same story she'd poured out in countless therapy session before condensing for Layla. She was invited to a party and she went. She met some guys. She had too much to drink. The last thing she remembered was one of them carrying her to the dance floor, twirling her around, and kissing her.

"The next morning, I woke up on a lounge chair outside. I had, well, in your grandfather's terms, I was no longer *pure.*" Her face was pinched with the effort to avoid tears.

Ian frowned, picturing it all, his mind providing the probable details of which she had, mercifully, no memory. He reached for his glass on the table and took a sizable swallow, shivering as it went down. "Do you remember how much you had to drink that night, at the party?"

"Two glasses of wine is what I remember. And then I passed out. Maybe I had more during the night? I don't remember. It really hit me fast."

Ian pointed to the glass in her hand. "How much of that have you had?"

"Maybe half, three-quarters?"

Ian nodded and held up his glass. "This is 100 proof moonshine, if not more. There's no *way* you got drunk on two glasses of wine if you can handle this stuff. You were drugged, Kristina. I would bet my life on it."

"Drugged! Richard wouldn't…" Suddenly, it all made sense. He'd been the one to get her drinks, no one else. That wink at his friend, what's-his-name. And the other guy. Her face went pale. *The three of them were in on it. Did all three?* No longer able to hold the tears back, she began to cry softly.

Ian gave in to instinct. He set his glass down and wrapped his arms protectively around Tina as she let years of self-doubt and self-loathing go. "It wasn't your fault," he whispered. "Whatever happened, it wasn't your fault. *Shhh.* It's okay, Kristina. It's okay."

Finally, she looked up into Ian's face, touched by the concern she saw there. "All this time, I thought I had messed up. The guy even spread rumors about me; at least I'm pretty sure he did. I barely made it to graduation or had the motivation to look for a job."

Ian gently smoothed a tendril of hair behind her ear. "What turned things around for you? You seem so confident now."

Tina smiled sadly. "I almost lost my sister and baby niece last year. It reminded me that life is short. It pushed me to get some help. A *lot* of therapy. A new start. New state, new job, new friends. But I'm not there yet. I've held onto a lot of negative thoughts. I've been kind of numb in some ways. Kept walls up."

"I," Ian began and stopped. His frown suddenly turned into a smile. "I was about to say that I would like you to consider me a friend and just realized that if my calculations were right about the New Moon celebration, it's after midnight now. Today is Atohuna, Friends Made ceremony. How's that for timing?" he asked softly.

As he gazed into her eyes, she drew in a breath. It wasn't the moonshine that was doing it, of that she was certain. Her heart was beating faster. Down… there… she felt moisture drip onto her thigh. She shifted her weight and tensed her muscles, experiencing excitement she had never felt before. To feel *anything* after all this time was nothing short of miraculous.

Ian's strong arms had trapped her own in his embrace. *He wants to be my friend.* Wouldn't any gentleman reach out to comfort a woman in distress? Amazed by her own boldness, Tina pulled her arms free and put them around Ian's neck, never once taking her eyes away from his. "Ian, please. Kiss me?"

Their mouths met as if every moment of the last day had been a slow percolation of desire. Without losing the connection, Ian stood and pulled Tina to her feet, his hands holding her tight this second, tenderly exploring her curves the next. Her own hands moved from his neck, to his back, to his buttocks. She pulled him tightly against her body with a moan. Breathless, their mouths parted, and for a second, they backed a few inches from each other, overwhelmed by the fury of what they had just experienced.

Ian's eyebrows lifted in question.

"Yes," she murmured. "Oh, yes."

The fire popped and sizzled as four hands unbuttoned, unzipped, pulled off and stepped out of every piece of clothing. They stood, skin to skin, kissing, exploring with their tongues. Ian took his kisses slowly across her face, down her neck, onto her chest. Cupping her breasts in both hands, he nuzzled each one, then took first one nipple, then the other, in his mouth, sucking gently, biting tenderly, until Tina thought she would scream with bliss.

All the while, her own hands traced his broad shoulders, his sculpted arms. When she reached for his chest, she let her fingers glide gently all around. He was smooth as a boy, but this was no boy. Except for his thick black mane, he had very little hair anywhere that she could tell, although she had yet to touch him... there.

He knelt low now, licking and kissing her stomach and abdomen, falling to his knees before her. Tina gasped as he reached behind her to hold her bottom firmly. His tongue found its way between the folds of her soft fur, masterfully stroking every inch of her, circling her little button. For years, she had been unable to conjure the slightest sensation there, but Ian was having no problem at all.

Just when she thought her knees would give way from sheer pleasure, Ian pulled her down to the mattress. They were both on their knees, hands furiously but lovingly moving as they kissed passionately. When Ian reached a hand between her legs, exploring gently, then earnestly, Tina reached between his muscular thighs. What she found made her draw in a breath. If this was to be her first real initiation into the wonders of manhood, Ian had to be the perfect specimen. She gripped the thick shaft of his cock with a moan that matched his, letting her hand explore its length. The tip was smooth as silk, in stark contrast to the quivering hardness attached.

In unison, the two lay down on the mattress, oblivious to the temperature, generating their own heat supply as Ian straddled her, spread her legs, and lifted her hips to meet him, rocking together for only a few minutes before her orgasm sent waves of euphoria throughout her body. Ian took his hands from behind her, grabbed her hands and held them over her head as he continued to thrust. Tina circled his waist with her legs and pulled him deeper and deeper until his body shuddered, and he let out a loud cry of release.

Ian raised his head, looking down at her, his breath slowing quickly after years of mountain hikes. He leaned down to kiss her sweetly on the mouth. His hips continued to rock ever so gently.

"So *that's* what all the commotion was about," Tina whispered. "I didn't know." Without even knowing she was moving, her hips began to rock with his. "What are you *doing?* Oh!"

"Nothing," he murmured. "Don't mind me, little Kristina. Don't. Mind. Me." As she climaxed again, more gently but also more profoundly, his thrusts sped up, taking her to the peak a third time. She burst into laughter as he exploded again within her and finally rolled over onto his back. They lay in the dying firelight.

"What's so funny?" he said finally.

Tina turned to face him. "You. You said not to mind you, but I'll bet if I don't, you'll spank me again—perhaps more gently this time." She laid her head back on the pillow and stared at the rough-hewn boards of the ceiling. "I had no idea it would feel this way. It was just so amazing! Thank you. It really was my first time, wasn't it? And it was perfect."

Ian kissed her again and got up to add wood to the fire. She watched him, drinking in the sight of his nakedness. He turned to face her, completely comfortable with her appreciative scrutiny.

"Ian," she said softly, pulling the covers around her. Without his heat next to her, she was suddenly chilled.

"Yes?"

"Is the Friends Made ceremony always this much fun?"

14

A Welcome Thaw

L ayla Henderson was beside herself with worry. The Weather Channel had been on every waking moment for days, and things finally looked a little more positive. When the phone rang, she prayed it was her sister with good news. Instead, it was Jessica.

"Have you heard anything yet?" Jessica asked.

"Not a word," Layla said with a sigh. "I'm about to come unglued. Poor Angela, she doesn't understand why her mommy's tied up in knots." Layla sighed again. "I'll let you know as soon as I do."

"Thanks. Mom and Chet are concerned as well, of course. But I'm sure she's fine. It's just hard not knowing, isn't it?" Jessica hoped to encourage her sister-in-law. "They said the power's been off in about a three-county area."

"I just wish I had somebody else's number down there. You can be *damn* sure I'll have a list after this little escapade. No way I'm going through this again," Layla said, sounding tired and cranky.

"How about some good news then?"

Layla sat down. "I'm listening."

Jessica told her that Worth had gone to Arizona and tracked down the men who were responsible for the grant money. "He says he's got what he hopes will be a solution for her. Some closure, anyway. At least she can know what really took place. But that's all he said. He flies home tonight."

Hundreds of miles away, Eleanor Rigby pulled her robe's sash tight and smiled at the man in her bed. She would put a pot of coffee on and see if perhaps phone service was restored. Not that she could call Tina, thanks to Frank and Jesse James here, but Will should be able to reach Ian if service was back on. At least he'd know about the tree in the road. She could find out how Tina was managing. It made her furious to think of what she'd been through these past days, and she didn't want to be furious. She stopped thinking about it, a surprisingly effective method for stress reduction she'd learned over the years.

Sunday night, she had called Will into her room to speak privately at greater length, but being in a bedroom alone with him had swept every argument from her mind. He'd stood there, forlorn, when she closed the door, clearly prepared for another tongue-lashing.

In the end, that's what she'd given him, in a way, she thought with a smile. Instead of scolding, she had blurted out, "Oh, Will. I missed you so much, how can I be angry with you now? Look at us!" She had walked straight into his arms. "We're eighty years old. Life is too short to waste another second. I'll never leave you again, if you'll have me. I promise."

Bill Cameron had held the love of his life, not as an old man, but as a fifteen-year-old again. After so many years, she felt just as good in his arms, just as right. It broke his heart to think that she'd been stolen away from him in the night, that their child had been ripped from her like that. But she was back. For however long he had left, she was his.

"Shall we go to bed, Nora?" he had said softly.

Nora had never had a shy bone in her body, but she had turned away from him and undressed behind the open closet door, slipping a heavy flannel gown over her head. "It's going to get cold tonight with no power," she'd said primly as she climbed under the covers. Atop the crocheted coverlet, she'd added a colorful, heavy quilt.

Looking at his sleeping figure now, she smiled, remembering his little speech. "I didn't plan on staying the night, so I'm afraid there are no pajamas to wear. I'll just sleep like this," he'd said, slipping into bed beside her. He had kissed her softly on the lips, his beard tickling her chin, and said, "Turn over, Nora. We can spoon the night away. I've been dreaming of that for sixty-five years."

Eleanor had nestled her back against his chest as he held her under the quilt, their legs bent parallel. "It's hard to believe, isn't it? To finally be together, just when time is so short."

Maybe time is short, but I don't remember that about him. *Lord, we had such a grand time together.* Eleanor had wiggled her bottom to meet his lap. "Mmm-mm. Let's go to sleep now. Talk more in the morning."

Eleanor touched her cheek, thinking of how sweetly he had stroked it in the dark. A little sadly, he had confessed that he wasn't sure he could do more than talk at his age. She had smiled in the darkness and kissed his fingers before wiggling her bottom against him with a bit more pressure. As she'd anticipated, there was a response. "And what do you call that poking me in the back, Will Cameron?"

His whole body had moved with a silent chuckle before he murmured, "Maybe I'm not about to die after all." He had proved his point last night.

Now, Eleanor tiptoed down the hallway and found Chip in

the kitchen. "I made a pot of coffee," he said. "Hope you don't mind. And I brought some more firewood in."

"Thank you, Chip. I hope you slept all right?"

He nodded but couldn't help grinning. "And you?"

"Yes, thank you," she said, pulling some yogurt and the creamer from the refrigerator quickly. "I'm afraid this is about it, other than the fresh fruit on the counter. If I had a good wood stove, we'd be in business."

"This is fine for me," Chip said, peering out the kitchen window. "'Snow's still almost a foot here, but it'll be a lot higher on the mountain, I'm afraid. Mr. Bill has a fine wood stove, though, so if Ian got back okay, Tina will have food for sure."

"If," Eleanor said softly, pouring a cup of coffee for herself.

They sat at the same table they'd played cards with Tina on so many happy evenings, each hoping their friend was safe, lost in their own thoughts and speculations.

"Did you save some for me, I hope?" Bill Cameron yawned as he came into view.

Yesterday morning, his clothing had obviously been slept in. Chip had inwardly complimented his boss's chivalric behavior. This morning, however, he was buttoning up his shirt. Chip got up to fix him a cup of coffee, seeing with a sideways glance the tender kiss Mr. Bill and Eleanor shared without embarrassment. He cleared his throat. "So, Eleanor. I'm right sorry about your baby, but I've been wondering if maybe we could track him down. Maybe they wouldn't allow it back then, but nowadays you can find most anybody. I'll bet Tina would help."

"If she's able," Eleanor said dryly.

"I'm going to apologize to her."

"If she doesn't sic the constable on you," she shot back.

"I don't know what got into me. I'm sorry, Nora," Bill said sheepishly. "It seemed like a good idea at the time. I didn't know there was going to be a dadgum blizzard or that a tree would fall down like that. Or that *someone* wouldn't have his chain saw?"

"Anyway," Chip interrupted loudly, sitting down across from them, "the more you remember, the easier it will be. Did they tell you anything at all?"

Eleanor made a face, thinking hard. "You're asking me about something that took place close to seventy years ago. I turned sixteen while I was carrying him, delivered after the New Year. That would have been, what, January of 1951?"

"Huh," said Chip. "Same year I was born. Same month, too. Ain't that a coincidence?"

Bill Cameron shook his head with a smirk. "I dare say a lot of young'uns were born in January of 1951."

Eleanor ignored them. "I gave birth in Chapel Hill, but the agency that came and took him was located in Raleigh. Some kind of state concern."

Chip tilted his head to one side, thinking intently. "Maybe we can track down all the boys adopted in Raleigh in January that year."

Eleanor shook her head. "I heard my parents talking one night. The baby was in foster homes before someone took him permanently. They didn't know their names, of course, and didn't want to. Some place with 'Creek' in the name where they lived. I started to look once, but there are too many towns in North Carolina that are some kind of Creek."

Chip stopped sipping his coffee and set down the cup. "Like Billy Creek?"

Eleanor shrugged. "Could be. Could be any of them. Why?"

"No reason."

Tina and Ian slept soundly through the night and made love again in the morning. When they lay back again, sighing happily in the aftermath, Tina said, "Well, good. I was afraid I'd dreamed it all last night." She turned to him and laid her hand across his chest. "Does it just keep getting better? I'm not sure it could."

Ian turned to face her for a kiss. "I don't know. I've never known it to be like this, Kristina Edwards. I have… had girl-friends. You aren't my first. I wish you were. But I've never had a woman respond to me the way you did. I've never felt a woman so ready for me or felt so wanted."

"Me either. Obviously." She made a face. "I could get used to this, Ian. But I don't think I'd ever take it for granted. I mean, what are the odds that a man would tie me up to meet his grandson and that I would fall…" Her voice drifted off. This was all so new to her. Would she frighten him away if she shared too much of her heart too fast?

"Tying you up. Hmm," Ian said with a leer. "That might be fun." Her words caught up with his brain. "You would fall how?"

Tina propped herself on an elbow and stroked his smooth chest. "You know what this reminds me of?"

"What?"

"An old musical my grandmother loved to watch on the classic movie station whenever it came on. She said our parents loved it too, *Seven Brides for Seven Brothers*. The oldest brother gets married and the other six kidnap the girls they're sweet on. When the daddies take off after them, there's a snow avalanche that blocks the pass. They have to live together—chastely—all winter."

Ian laughed. "Recent events have been the opposite of chastity, thankfully. So what happens when they can get through the pass?"

Tina closed her eyes, seeing the movie in her mind. "The

married brother's wife has had a baby in the meantime, and all the other girls say it's theirs, so the daddies will make them get 'hitched'."

Ian played with the hair cascading over her breasts and traced a path down to her stomach, walking his fingers slowly downward. "Are you asking me to keep you up here all winter? I think I could manage that."

Tina pulled the top blanket and wrapped it around her as she stood, laughing. She ran to the porch window and pulled open the heavy curtain. It was a beautiful day. "Ian! It's gone down quite a bit."

Ian joined her, wrapping his arms around her from behind. "I'll get dressed and scout around. How about you melt some snow while I'm gone, make some coffee? Rustle up some eggs and bacon?"

Tina made a face. "I've never cooked on a wood stove. Maybe *I* should get dressed and scout around and *you* rustle up breakfast."

Ian laughed, whipping her around for a kiss. She let the blanket fall, despite the chill in the air. "Brrr," she said, burying her head in his chest.

"Brrr is right. Let's *both* get dressed. I'll help you with breakfast, and then we'll both go outside—if I can find you some boots."

As they ate their bacon and eggs, Tina tried to fill in the gap of knowledge regarding the Cameron men. "You've been gone, you said. Where have you been?"

Ian squeezed her knee under the table. "After college, I took some post-grad courses, scouted out jobs, went to interviews. My degree is in social work, with a minor in public relations."

Tina giggled. "You've got a PhD in *private* relations." She blushed. After years of being closed off, it was like a dam had burst, and the rush of the river was exhilarating. Realizing that she'd likely been drugged and raped was horrible, but it wasn't as horrible as the belief that she had brought it all on herself. Her expression turned serious. "Would you cut my hair?"

He frowned. "I love your hair. You really do remind me of Rapunzel."

"I'm serious, Ian. See, for all this time, I've been walled off, in a tower of my own making, just like Rapunzel. I didn't think I *could* leave. No one was coming to rescue me, and even if someone had, I would have pushed him away." She smiled. "Until you. I let down my hair and you climbed up—"

"I climbed *you?*" Tina threw a spoon and hit him in the head.

"Ow!" he yelped.

Tina's eyes were serious. "It's symbolic. You don't have to cut much. Please?"

Shaking his head in protest, Ian scooted his chair back and went into the bathroom. He came out carrying a small box. "Grandfather cuts his own hair, so at least there are proper scissors."

"What is up with that?" she said scornfully. "He owns a mountain, for heaven's sake. He takes my rent money every month and Lord only knows how many others. Has he always been a miser? And how does he afford to live up here anyway? I'd think the taxes alone would be astronomical on this much property."

Ian shrugged. "Winning the lottery helped."

Tina was drinking a sip of coffee and spit it out with a cough. "Whaaat? When?"

"Put all your hair over the chair back and sit up perfectly straight and still," Ian directed. "North Carolina got the lottery about fifteen years ago, and my grandfather was one of the first big winners. Poplar Gap was struggling, but he invested in the community, kept things alive. He also invested in gold."

"Gold?" She could hear the scissors snipping behind her

and hoped he knew what he was doing. *I hope this wasn't the dumbest idea I ever had.*

"He did quite well, actually. He's got it stashed away some-where up here. One of the reasons for all the traps. He doesn't like banks. There."

Gold in them thar hills. I was right. Tina ran her fingers through her hair, at first frightened by the result. Ian had trimmed about a foot, but it was still long. This would be less trouble to take care of and to style, though. She turned her head from side to side, letting her hair swish back and forth. "You like?"

"No," Ian said with a straight face. "I hate to tell you this, but shorter hair means I will never touch you again." He kissed her. "You are even more beautiful."

A faint noise could be heard overhead. They both were immediately still, straining to hear. "Where's it coming from?" Tina whispered. "What is it?"

Without a word, Ian bounded up the stairs and opened the door of his bedroom. The noise stopped, but Tina could hear Ian's voice. He came out wearing a broad grin, holding his cell phone to his ear and pointing to it, as if she couldn't see. "We're about to go out and check out the well," he was telling someone. "Right, see where the pipe's broken. Pipes, glue, brush, sure. You're kidding. Chain saw, check. We'll be down as soon as we can."

Tina waved at him furiously, trying to get his attention. "What?" he mouthed, then, "hold on."

"They can call Layla! Let her know I'm okay. The charge is probably gone, but if they plug it in, there's no lock on the screen. Layla Henderson, in the contact list. Please! Thank you so much."

"Do you want to talk to Grandfather yourself?"

She shook her head with a sudden scowl. "What I have to say to him should be said in person."

Tina put on as many layers of clothing from the trunk as she could, over which she put on her own heavy coat, dirty jeans, gloves and hat. By this time, Ian was dressed as well. "I look like the Michelin man." She laughed.

"As long as you're warm. I've got to pick up some tools from the shed out back, then it's a hike. Ready?"

At the well house, Ian found and repaired a broken pipe that had frozen and popped apart. Tina handed him tools and oohed and ahhed over his work. She gazed up toward the mountaintop, where she could just see the cell tower periscoping above the pines. Ian's pick-up truck was, as he'd said, parked on the gravel road near the well, snow still piled in the bed.

"If you want to wait in the truck, I'll go back to the house, get the chain saw, and make sure the fires are out." He handed her the keys. "Start 'er up and turn the heat on. I won't be long."

Soon, they were driving down the mountain, Tina's head leaning on Ian's shoulder as he drove. It must be Tuesday, she thought. *I need to call Ms. Clark.* She turned on the radio and found a station with frequent news updates. County schools would remain closed until next week, as much of the area remained without power, but progress was being made. Temperatures were expected to continue to rise slowly, with no precipitation in the forecast.

The truck stopped at the fallen tree on her road. Ian got the chain saw out and was about to begin the work of cutting it up when Tina shook her head and took it from him, replacing it in the bed of the truck. "Come with me first," she said.

"Go easy on the old man," Ian said as they walked down the road to Eleanor's, hand in hand. "He thinks he's dying, but there's no need for you get a head start with that."

As they came around the corner, Tina dropped his hand and moved further away from him. "I'm just going to tell him what's in my heart, Ian. I have to do that after what he put me through."

"Understood," Ian said, pointing ahead. "Here's our welcoming committee."

Bill Cameron, Eleanor and Chip stood on the porch, their faces grim. Ian had said nothing about Tina on the phone, other than to call her sister. Tina could tell from their expressions that Mr. Cameron and Chip were prepared for the worst. Instead, Tina broke into a jog and threw her arms around a very surprised old man. "Thank you," she murmured. "Thank you, thank you, thank you."

Ian was all smiles as he walked up and shook Eleanor's hand, then Chip's, while Tina hugged everyone through her tears.

Eleanor was the first to break the reunion up. "Let's let these men get to work, honey. You and I can go inside, and you can tell me *all* about it."

Back to School

T ina's SUV was still in the shop, so Chip ran her into Humphrey every day, with Ian picking her up in the afternoon, often staying the night with her. Despite her resolve to keep Chip at a distance, feeling betrayed by him, it was difficult. He was such an affable guy, her first friend there, and—a big factor –his actions had directly led to her meeting Ian and falling in love, something she had thought impossible.

This morning, Principal Clark spoke with a parent as Chip eased his truck to the curb. "Who is *that*?" he asked appreciatively. Ellen Clark was animated as she talked to whomever she was speaking with through an open car window. Although they couldn't hear what she was saying, it was obvious that she was both passionate and pleased about her topic of conversation.

Tina raised her eyebrows at Chip. *Why hadn't I thought of this before?* It was true, she had assumed the principal was married when she first arrived at school in late August, but over the months, she'd learned that Ellen Clark was a widow whose husband had died in Afghanistan. Her children were grown. Two of her grandchildren attended school, riding daily with

Mama Clark. Very few secrets were kept in a small town like Humphrey for long.

Tina sniffed innocently. "Would you like me to introduce you? It'll only take a minute. I'm a little early."

As Principal Clark waved goodbye to the parent and then waved at the truck, the two of them got out. "Good morning, Principal Clark!" Tina called. "I'd like you to meet someone."

The woman was dressed professionally, Chip noticed, and carried a few extra pounds in exactly the places he enjoyed most, top and bottom. As she walked to meet them, she pulled her trench coat tighter against the November chill and looked up at the sky. "Think we'll get snow for Thanksgiving?"

"Almanac says it'll be a bad winter, but we might have a little more of a break. Ma'am," he said, tipping an invisible hat as he extended his hand. "Chip Murphy, ma'am."

"Ellen Clark, Mr. Murphy. But please, call me Ellen." She smiled. "And you are—" *Someone would have told me if Tina was involved with this man,* she thought out of habit, always keeping tabs on possible issues at school. *A bit old for her, anyway. My money's on the handsome man who's been picking her up.* It was against her upbringing and experience to consider she might be involved with both men at once, but these days—

"My first friend in Poplar Gap," Tina chimed in, interrupting her thoughts. "He helped me move in and we've been friends ever since. Such a big help." No need for her boss to know the whole *Seven Brides* fiasco.

"Very good, Mr. Murphy. Tina is one of our finest teachers, with one of our most challenging classes." It was bitterly cold.

She insisted on wearing dresses to work, and her legs, though covered with heavy tights, were freezing. She tried not to be too obvious but glanced at her watch out of years of the same routine. "Oh, it's almost time for the first bell," she said.

"You ladies have a wonderful day. Nice to meet you," Chip said. "Ian'll be here at four, Tina. We playin' cards with Eleanor?"

Tina nodded, and the two women walked toward the school entrance as his truck drove off. "Chip works for Bill Cameron, managing all his rentals, keeping them maintained, doing other jobs for him." *Like kidnapping.*

"With all the property that man owns, Mr. Murphy must stay busy," Principal Clark mused. She murmured a "Thank you" as Tina held the door open for her. "Is Eleanor his wife?"

Tina smiled and shook her head. "She's my next door neighbor. Chip lives behind me. The three of us used to play cards a lot in the evenings, but now my... boyfriend sounds a little juvenile, doesn't it? My significant other? This is all new to me! Ian is Mr. Cameron's grandson. The man who's been picking me up. Anyway, Ian plays cards with us too."

"He is *hot*," the principal said with a wink. "And Mr. Murphy's not bad himself." The first bell was heard throughout the campus. "I'll bet he could ring *my* bell," she said softly as she made the turn to her office.

Tina laughed as she walked to her classroom. *Well, I swanny.*

Thanksgiving break would be here before she knew it, but Tina was pleased with her class' progress.

"You're doing so well!" she told the students each day. The students had enjoyed their week off for snow, but these were kids who functioned better with structure. They were glad to be back with Miss Tina, Miz Martha, and the aide, Miss Betty

Lou. If snack wasn't exactly at ten, or if a picture hung off-kilter on the wall, someone was sure to mention it.

Tina's phone rang as she hung her coat on its peg in the classroom. Everyone had a specific space, even the teachers. *Layla.* "Hey! You caught me just in time. The first bell just rang, and kids'll be here any second. What's up?"

Layla sounded excited. "Do you remember Worth Vincent? Jessica's husband?"

"Sure! Shaved head, beard. Good-looking."

When they'd met at her house, "Kristina" hadn't indicated she noticed such details, more evidence her sister had gone through a radical transformation, even more so now.

"That's the one. He's a magazine editor, you know. And he wants to bring some folks to your school to discuss a project."

Tina was confused. "My school? I can give you the principal's number. Her name is Ellen Clark, and sh—"

"No, he insisted they speak with you, personally. Worth will be at the meeting too. Would Thanksgiving week suit you?"

"Sure. I mean the kids won't be here, but I could show them around the campus. I'm sure Ms. Clark wouldn't mind if I tell her first. She might want to be—"

"Worth was adamant about that. Just you. It's a *stipulation* with the men coming," her sister interrupted again.

The second bell rang, and children of all ages scurried and laughed in the hallway. "I've got to go, Lay, but sure. Tell Worth that will be fine. Do I need to find them places to stay, or—"

Tina could hear Angela's singsong baby talk in the background. Layla was convinced her "words" meant something. "All you need to do is meet with them. Worth will handle the rest. I love you! Have a great day." *Click.*

"Well, well," Tina said aloud to the empty classroom. It was Martha's turn to meet the class at the bus and walk them there. The aide was out with a cold. Her eyes swept the classroom.

She had bought several things with her own money, but there was so much she'd like to do for the kids. She'd seen her grandparents scrape and save all their lives, and she knew she should be thrifty with the remainder of the mysterious grant, but there were so many needs. She took a deep breath as the door opened.

The day begins. "Good morning, Jeffrey!"

Eleanor had taught them to play Canasta, and tonight, it was the men against the women. Since both Ian and his grandfather would be there, Chip had offered to stay home with Blue, but they insisted. "I don't like cards all that much, anyway," Bill said. "Now, chess! That's a real game. I'll just watch and read or something."

Now that power was fully operational again, the modest fire in the fireplace added more atmosphere than heat. Ian had cut the fallen tree into a treasure trove of firewood, stacked neatly at the various houses to dry for next winter. The stickies Eleanor had showed Tina how to make were almost ready, the cinnamon smell filling the air.

"Your deal, Chip," Ian said. "Kristina tells me you met her principal this morning. Said the woman was *quite* impressed with you."

Chip made a noise as he deftly shuffled the cards. "She's a lot of woman, just the way I like 'em." He dealt the cards with the speed and accuracy of someone who has been doing it for many years. "I should teach you ladies how to play poker. Ian, you play?"

"No thank you," Eleanor interrupted with a sniff. "If Daddy hadn't loved to gamble, I wouldn't have had to marry Mr. Rigby."

Chip drawled, "I wasn't thinking of playing for money,

Miss High-and-Mighty. We could play for pennies or match-sticks. Your turn."

Bill called in from the sofa, "I suppose we could play strip poker if you'd rather."

The friends all laughed. It was only a matter of time before the older couple got married. He'd told her it was high time for her to have the Cameron name, but definite plans had yet to be made. The couple discreetly shared a bed, either on the mountain or here, more often than not. Anyone in Poplar Gap who assumed they were too old for anything but cuddling were… incorrect.

When the timer went off, Tina went to take the stickies out of the oven, carefully sliding them onto a plate with a spatula. Their aroma reminded her of her childhood. She'd rolled out pie crust dough on a marble slab, slathered it with soft butter, sprinkled it heavily with cinnamon and sugar, then rolled the dough up, sliced it, and baked the little rounds to gooey deliciousness.

"Bring the milk, too," Eleanor called. "Nothing better with stickies."

Bill joined them at the table to eat. "So, Chip. Nora and I have been wanting to ask you about something."

"What's that?" Chip shifted his cards in his hand, grouping them together to the best advantage.

Eleanor opened her mouth and closed it several times before finally saying, "Will, maybe this isn't the best time?"

Tina and Ian exchanged a look. "If you'd like to talk privately, we could call it a night," she offered, halfway hoping they would take her up on it. The thought of sliding into bed with Ian was much more appealing than Canasta.

"The night of the snow, Nora was telling us about our baby, that he fostered in a few homes in Raleigh before an adoption by a couple from somewhere else."

"Yep," Chip said, studying his hand. "I remember."

"The town had Creek in the name. You're from Billy Creek, right?"

"Yep."

"And you were born in January of '51, right?"

"Yep." Chip sat upright and shook his head. "I see where you're goin' with this, and I admit I thought as much that night for about five minutes. But it's too much of a coincidence."

"You said your family used to come out here of a summer, for vacation," Bill continued. "Do you think they might have *known* where your parents were and wanted to find them for you?"

Tina's heart began to race. *Wouldn't that be awesome?* "I know someone who's coming here at Thanksgiving. His family owns a magazine, has lots of connections. Maybe he could find something out for sure? I mean, how cool would that be?"

Chip shook his head. "You'uns want to go off on a wild goose chase, you have my blessing." He felt bad for dismissing them—this was their love child in question, after all. "I mean, I hope you find your young'un, I really do. That'll be a happy day, if it comes. I'll be jumpin' up and dancin' right along with you, Mr. Bill."

Thanksgiving Surprises

Tina was nestled in the warm bed, enjoying her nightly phone call with Layla. "I'm sending Jessica with Worth tomorrow, to spy out this Ian guy," her sister said with a laugh. "Just so you know. She's to report back to me as soon as she can."

Tina rolled her eyes. "I would expect nothing less. I'm hoping to talk him into coming for a visit at Christmas if that's all right."

"All right! That's great! You should see Angela. She's almost walking. She'll let go of the sofa for a second, look around to see if we're watching, and then sit down on her bottom. It's the cutest thing you've ever seen."

Tina was curled up in her comforter, a leg lazily stretched across Ian's. When she reached a hand between his legs, he looked up from his reading with a smirk. "Talk to your sister," he whispered, "so we can get on with things."

Tina made kiss lips at him. "What was that, Layla?" She made a face at Ian, as if the distraction had been his fault.

Layla's voice was louder, and Tina could hear a commotion

in the background. "I said I need to go. Talk to you tomorrow." *Click.*

Tina plugged her phone into the charger and laid it on the bedside table. Ian was halfway through a Ferrol Sam book Eleanor had loaned her. It was a great book, but she didn't feel guilty one bit about talking him out of it. Without a word, she slithered down beneath the covers until her head was at the foot of the bed, licking Ian's toes and kissing his feet. Straddling his legs backwards, she rubbed his feet, hitting all the pressure points she knew he appreciated as she nibbled his calves and pressed her breasts onto them. She heard the book snap shut.

Ian held her hips in his hands. "Oh, you are in perfect position for another spanking," he murmured. "Have you been naughty lately?" He swatted her bottom sharply, then caressed her. "That was just in case. But is there anything you need to tell me?"

Tina chuckled softly as she pulled the coverlet off her head and sat up, looking over her shoulder. She held up a hand for scout's honor. "I promise I haven't trespassed on the mountain and I will never run away from you again."

"In that case, I have a better use for this position." Ian pushed her down on all fours as he slipped his legs out from under her and stood up by the bed, pulling her closer to the edge. They had spent one night in her twin bed before heading to the closest furniture store an hour away. The four-poster frame they'd bought with the queen mattress was high.

When Ian had asked the salesman who'd helped them to add risers to the bill, Tina had questioned him. "I'm fairly tall," was all he'd said, giving her a look that made her blush with understanding.

She turned her head to smile at him now as he reached beneath her, massaging her breasts tenderly yet firmly. Tina pushed her bottom back against him and he guided himself in.

Ian walked his hands back to her soft fur and made little circles with his fingers as he thrust his penis deeper and deeper. After several minutes, Tina cried hoarsely, "I want to see you."

Without a word, Ian slid himself from her, flipping her roughly on her back. With strong arms, he lifted her and positioned her further onto the mattress so that her head was at the foot of the bed and he could use the headboard to push his feet against. He was so tall that he towered over her, cushioning her head with his arms. As her hands scratched softly, then harder, on his back, Tina thought he would buck her off the bed completely, so energetic were his thrusts. She felt the wave of bliss rise in glorious crescendo as his own climax took over. They both cried out.

Ian stared at her as his hips slowed their rocking, not ready to stop altogether. "I love being inside you, beautiful Kristina."

"It's my favorite thing in the world too," Tina said, tightening her inner muscles around him. "Can you feel that?"

He leaned down to kiss her passionately, growing within her again. "But maybe you're ready for sleep?" he whispered.

"I've been asleep all my life," she said, wrapping her legs around his waist. "You finally woke me up."

———

Tuesday morning, Ian insisted on riding with Tina to the school in Humphrey. Ellen Clark had made arrangements for the main door to be unlocked by nine-thirty. Worth Vincent and his companions were to arrive at ten.

"Really, you don't need to do that," Tina had countered. "Don't you have some hunting to do for Thanksgiving? I'll be fine. I've met Worth. He's a great guy, really. I'm sure this is legit. I have no idea what it could be about, but I'll be fine."

Regardless, Ian went along, promising to sit in the lobby if she preferred. She'd nervously turned on the light in the conference room, found bottles of water in case anyone was thirsty, and wished ten o'clock would get there.

It did, along with Worth and six men. They nodded to Ian as he stood and extended a hand. He had a description of Worth, so his was the hand he shook first. "Ian Cameron, sir. I'll take you gentlemen to Kristina." It was obvious to him that only Worth was comfortable with the visit.

Worth beamed. "So you're the man we've heard so much about. My wife and I would love to take you and Kristina to dinner tonight if you're available."

Ian frowned. "With ev–"

Before anyone else could speak, Worth held up a hand to cut him off. "These gentlemen are heading to the airport as soon as our meeting is over. They have… business to attend to elsewhere.

Ian led the group down the darkened hallway to where light streamed from the conference room. Tina stood when the group entered and then just as quickly sat down in one of the chairs. She looked, for all the world, as if she had seen a ghost.

Sensing a concerned question regarding her welfare, Worth smiled at Ian. "She'll be fine, I promise. Would you excuse us?"

Tina swallowed, gazing at the faces of the men. The three younger ones faced her, while the three older men stood off to one side. Her head was spinning. The room was spinning. Worth handed her a bottle of water. "Let's get started, shall we?"

He cleared his throat. "Kristina Edwards, it has been two years, so no doubt you still remember your college mates, Richard Barrows, Todd Bailey, Junior, and Mitch O'Day. Over there, we have *Everett* Barrows, Todd Bailey, *Senior*, and *Clarence* O'Day." The older men acknowledged her with little nods and bows, while the younger trio stared at the table.

Worth continued, sweeping his hand to the standing men. "Or as you might know them, The Exagorà Foundation."

Tina gasped. "The grant? It was you?"

Everett Barrows cleared his throat. "It was. But we didn't fly all this way and drive all over creation to exchange pleasantries, young lady. These boys have something to say, and then we have a proposal." He waited. "Richard?"

Richard was still handsome, Tina thought, but he had acquired an air of something unattractive, although she wasn't sure what it was. *Entitlement? Laziness? Hard to tell.*

"I'm sorry," he murmured.

Worth inclined his ear toward the table. "What's that? I didn't quite make it out."

Richard glared at him. "I'm sorry!" he shouted, then he turned and looked at Tina directly. "I'm sorry," he said with all the sincerity he could muster.

"For what?" Tina asked. Everything she had learned from Elizabeth, and from Ian, and from her own growth, returned to infuse her with strength. "What did you do, that requires an apology? *Dick.*"

Tina got up from her chair and walked around the room as she spoke, every word empowering her to say the next. "You told *me* that I had had too much to drink that night and that I behaved badly at the frat party, *Dick*. I *embarrassed* you, you said. We had no future, you said. Your coach looked me up at my *job*, *Dick*, and asked if that's how I was raised!"

Six heads dropped in chagrin, and Worth wished he had a medal to put around Tina's neck.

Tina waited until she had every man's attention. "I was humiliated. Look at me! All of you! I was talked about. I very nearly lost my job and didn't graduate because I was so ashamed of myself." Tina crossed her arms protectively and grew quiet. "What really happened that night?"

Richard Barrows looked at his father as if for help. "Answer her, Richard," his father said, an edge in his voice. "The truth. The whole truth, and nothing but the truth, so help you God and any help you expect from me for the rest of your life!"

Worth cleared his throat, catching Tina's eye. Softly, he asked, "Would you like for me to wait outside?"

Tina smiled sadly and shook her head.

Richard sighed and looked at Todd and Mitch, shaking his head. "Now or never, fellows." He turned to Tina but continued to look at the table. "It was a dare. We thought it would be fun to make it with a virgin. Not many of those left on campus, but you were… different. You stood out. You were sweet and wholesome and studied all the time. We weren't sure, of course, not yet, anyway."

In the corner, the trio's fathers made noises of contempt and regret.

"Mitch got hold of a fast-working drug. I was supposed to ask you out."

"And Todd?"

"Todd kept you distracted while I went for the wine and drugged it."

"Go on," Tina said. She and Ian thought they knew what had happened, but they had only discussed generalities. Hearing the reality was harder.

Richard let out a long sigh. The others squirmed visibly, unable to make eye contact with her. *Oh Lord, maybe just one of them,* she thought. *Maybe one and the others watched. That's bad enough, but—*

"You got loopy pretty fast and wanted to dance, so I picked you up. At some point, I kissed you. As soon as I saw you were passed out cold, I carried you upstairs to Mitch's room. I, um, I went first."

Tina cleared her throat, hoping her voice came out steady as she sat back down and folded her hands in front of her on the table. "Todd and Mitch… watched?"

They nodded. Todd spoke next. "I went next." He looked

up at Tina. "I am so sorry." He looked at the other two with tears in his eyes. "They didn't know it, but I was a virgin that night, too. I…" He began to sob. "…Oh, God, I am so sorry. I'd do anything if I could take it back."

No one said anything as he sobbed quietly. Worth handed him a tissue from a box on a nearby bookshelf. The room was silent otherwise.

From the corner of the room, Clarence O'Day coughed.

Mitch nodded. "I went last. I was rougher with you than they were. I… had anger issues towards women and… I'm also sorry."

Tina stared at the men. *Words matter.* "You're *sorry*. You're all sorry it happened. Well, no surprise here, so am I." She frowned. "Is that all you came to tell me? Don't get me wrong; I'm thankful to know the truth. I'm thankful to know that it wasn't *my* doing, *my* poor choices, all the lies I believed for so long. The lies you *let* me believe."

Todd was the first to speak again. "We can't undo what we did, Kristina, but maybe one day you can forgive us for drugging you and lying to you, and… and raping you. Oh, man, that word always turns my stomach." He looked at his one-time friends and partners in crime. "We are rapists, plain and simple. *We raped her.* We didn't even give her the *chance* to say no or to fight back. We were *complete* cowards. Idiots." He turned back to Tina. "I understand if you can't forgive us. I just hope that one day you can. That's all." He glared at Richard, then Mitch.

Richard said quietly, "Please forgive me for hurting you, Kristina."

"Me, too," said Mitch. "It was the worst mistake of my life. Please forgive me."

Tina looked at the misery in their eyes. If it hadn't been for that night and all that followed, she would still be teaching out west. She would be happy, she assumed, but she wouldn't have found Ian. She may never have found love. "Richard. Todd. Mitch. All I can say is that I will try."

She took a deep breath. "Well. I guess you guys have a plane to catch." She looked up at Worth, who—oddly, she thought– was grinning from ear to ear.

"Not just yet," he said with a little wink. "Gentlemen? I believe the trustees of the Exagorà Foundation have something to add."

Everett Barrows stepped forward with a folded check in his hand. "*Exagorà* means 'redemption' in Greek, and that is what we wanted to do, Miss Edwards, with that grant, to find redemption for our sons. We, ah, realize now that we greatly underestimated the damage that they, uh, caused. Mr. Vincent was, um, *kind* enough to find us and point things out more clearly." He was a businessman, and as he got down to business, Tina could see him relax more.

Everett explained that they had hoped the grant would take care of her personal needs. "I understand therapy and a move, some other things, were available that perhaps would not have been?"

Tina nodded, crossing her arms, now in defiance. *They thought they could buy me? Am I supposed to just forget it all now? Is that the idea?*

Everett continued. "We immediately dissolved the foundation, but Mr. Vincent convinced us to, well, the foundation is alive and well, and what we propose is adopting your class. At this school, or wherever you may go in the future."

Tina made a face, confused. "I don't understand."

Everett gestured around the room. "The class, the school. Forever. We've put money in trust so that wherever you teach, there will be funds to do whatever you think would be best for your students. Or you could use the trust for startup funds and build a whole school, for that matter. Whatever you want."

He handed her the check. "This is for this calendar year,

Miss Edwards. Funds are accruing interest. The foundation will send the same amount, or more, each year until you tell us to stop. Our lawyers will send you some forms to fill out, beneficiaries, what happens if you predecease us, all the nit-picky details of this kind of thing, you understand."

Tina slowly unfolded the check and drew in a breath. She looked at the men in disbelief.

Todd Bailey, Sr., spoke up. "We must also ask for your forgiveness, Miss Edwards. Our sons were not raised to be rapists, but we have to acknowledge our own failures along the way, and especially concerning the grant. At the time, you could have pressed charges, and we… our motives were not entirely unselfish."

Clarence O'Day had a look that said *I guess I have to say something too, dammit.* "Please forgive us, Miss Edwards. We put what was, in retrospect, too low a value on you and your state of mind, your future. If you *ever* need anything, anything at all, please contact me personally." He handed her his card, which prompted the others to follow suit.

Worth clapped his hands. "Fabulous! Anyone have anything else they want to say? No? Then let's allow Miss Edwards and Mr. Cameron to enjoy the rest of their day. I'll send you off to the airport, and Tina? How about I send a car for you and Ian at, say, six?"

That night at dinner, between several delicious courses at one of Asheville's most exclusive resorts, Tina and Jessica caught up on news while Worth discussed another pressing matter with Ian. Shortly after he'd made arrangements to come there, he told Ian, Tina had emailed a rather strange request. "She had the notion that I was a man who could get things done," Worth said modestly. "And in her case, and in this one, it turns out she was right. Take this with you and look at it when you have time." He handed Ian a thick manila envelope that was sealed.

"No wine for you, Jessica?" Tina asked. "Oh, right! Layla told me you're expecting. Congratulations!"

Jessica beamed at Worth. "We couldn't be happier."

Ian laid a hand on Tina's leg. Despite the cold, she'd worn a wrap-around dress. She was suddenly grateful for the floor-length white tablecloth as Ian's hand found the slit in the fabric and caressed her leg, silky inside thigh-high stockings. He moved his hand up, and up, stopping at the top of the stocking. He looked lovingly at her. She warned him with her eyes and leaned over to whisper in his ear, "I am having a difficult enough time focusing on the conversation as it is, Mr. Cameron. Don't you dare—"

Ian smiled then turned to Worth with a question about the magazine. As he chatted, his hand found the silk of her panties and pressed against it rhythmically.

I'm about to lose my mind, Tina thought. *Damn Indians and their stealth. Jessica and Worth have no idea.* She let out a little cry.

"Are you okay?" Ian asked innocently.

"I just, um, need to use the restroom," she said with a sniff and stood. Ever the gentlemen, Ian and Worth stood as well, followed quickly by Jessica.

"Girls never go to the restroom alone, you know," Jessica said with a laugh and guided Tina in the right direction. As they walked, Jessica whispered, "That scamp practically had me undressed under the table! And me pregnant, too."

It was very late when the driver let Tina and Ian out of the car and bid them goodnight at her house. One day they would move in together, but for the time being, they went back and forth between her house and his room in the cabin on the mountain. Weekdays, it made sense to be closer to the school, but weekends were spent hiking and hunting. Ian was even teaching Tina to shoot.

Tina yawned as they went inside. Tomorrow, she would pack a bag and spend the rest of the week with him on the mountain. His grandfather wanted to spend the week with Eleanor, so they'd have the cabin all to themselves. The four of them would gather at Eleanor's for Thanksgiving dinner, but Chip had an invitation to join Ellen Clark and her children in Humphrey.

As Tina got undressed, Ian dropped the manila envelope on the bed. "What's that?" Tina asked.

Frowning, Ian tore open one edge and rifled through the papers and photographs inside. "Well, I'll be damned," he muttered and stared up at Tina.

"What?" Her eyes were wide. "I asked Worth to do some digging. Is that—"

"A baby boy, born to Eleanor Bradshaw, January 10, 1951. Adopted by Ezekiel and Maude Murphy of Billy Creek in March the same year. Kristina. This means that Chip is my uncle!"

Tina did a little victory dance around the room. "I guess he'll finally have to give up that Mr. Bill nonsense! 'Dad' sounds so much better."

Some Years Later

Kristina Cameron took the shovel from her husband Ian, put one foot up onto the step and pushed hard. She extracted a sizable bounty of rich brown earth and threw it ceremoniously. Everyone who was gathered on the fine spring day applauded. She handed the shovel to her sister, who repeated the procedure to repeated fanfare. When Ian crouched over expectantly, Kristina put her niece Angela on his broad shoulders.

Principal Ellen Clark-Murphy held the microphone and smiled out at the audience. "Be it known that on this day, we break ground for the new wing of Humphrey K-12, the Edwards Memorial Special Education Building. Jeffrey, would you like to do the honors next?"

Jeffrey Wilson, the newest aide in the autism department, grinned and took the shovel from his former teacher's sister. It had taken a while to get used to all the name changes—Miss Tina, then Miss Kristina. Miss Edwards, then Mrs. Cameron. He had kept a chart so that he would remember. Now he put his foot down and dug up a scoop of earth.

"Miz Cameron!" he shouted happily. "We did it!"

Kristina Cameron nodded at Jeffrey and then gazed out on

the crowd of people, people she had grown to love over the last few years. Pop Cameron stood arm in arm with Eleanor, more stoop-shouldered, perhaps, than when he'd tied her up in the cabin alone that long ago October, but still going strong.

Eleanor, in turn, looked up with pride and joy into the face of her son, the principal's husband. He had been ripped away from her as an infant, but now that she had Chip back in her life, she was making up for lost time.

Mr. and Mrs. Worth Vincent stood in the back, content that they'd had a part to play in the joyous occasion. Each parent held the hand of a child. Jessica squeezed Worth's hand between them and mouthed the words "*Thank you.*" Had it not been for him, much of this would never have happened. He mouthed the words back at his wife. Her coming into his life, and into his heart, had had every bit as much to do with the day's success.

Tina shook her head at the love and support she witnessed. *I have never been this happy, this complete, in my entire life,* she thought, lifting her eyes to the sky, a beautiful Carolina blue. *Mom and Dad, I know you're pleased. We miss you. We love you.*

Not only was the Exagorà Foundation's money going toward a new wing of the school, it had enabled her to start a non-profit in Humphrey to help victims of sexual violence. She had been both sobered and pleased by the response.

Suddenly, she knew what she must do.

Later that night, Ian came up behind her and nuzzled her neck as she sat writing something at the table in the cabin on the mountain. His grandfather and Eleanor had chosen to live in Eleanor's house. At their age, they felt it was more prudent to be closer to civilization and any necessary medical care.

Chip had moved to Humphrey to live with Ellen, but he

visited his relatively new and multiple extended families often. One of Ellen's sons had moved into Chip's old house with his wife and daughter, who happily adopted "Papa Will" and "Nana Nora" as her own. And there was still plenty of room on the mountain for Ian and Kristina's children, grandchildren, and beyond, should God bless them in that way. So far, it was just the two of them, but they did hope—and provide opportunity as often as they could.

"I'll be there in a minute," Kristina said, covering her writing with an arm. "Promise."

As Ian went to bed, Kristina finished her task, carefully addressed six envelopes, and turned her paper over. Tomorrow, she would make copies at work and drop them in the mail. She doubted she would get any response, but that didn't matter. *I'm doing this for* me.

During the night, Ian got up for a drink of water from the refrigerator. As he opened the door, the dim light shone onto the table. He remembered his first meal there with Kristina, fried rabbit. He smiled in the semi-darkness and left the door open so that he could see what she'd been working on.

Dear gentlemen, her letter read.

I've given things a lot of thought since we last met. I've learned more about mindfulness, too. When I try to view what transpired at that frat party as if seeing it all in a mirror, it has no power to hurt me. I am able to understand the negativity that drove you, that controlled me. I also see how it all affected me positively, something I wouldn't have thought possible at one time.

I hope that you have learned as much from that night as I have. I hope that you have grown and changed. If you still struggle with anger or shame or guilt, I encourage you to seek counseling. I can recommend someone out your way if you need a name.

The Exagorà Foundation's finances continue to bring fulfillment and educational opportunities to many. In a roundabout but profound way, what you intended for your own benefit—and for my hurt—has brought me more joy than you can imagine. For that reason, and because I do not deserve to carry an ounce of anger for even one more second, I forgive you. I release you from guilt. I thank you.

The letter was signed: *Sincerely, Kristina Edwards Cameron.*

Ian's eyes filled with tears. *What an incredible woman she is.* He was about to lay the paper down when he had a thought and picked up the pen.

Gentlemen, he added at the bottom, *thank you for sending Kristina my way. It has been my greatest pleasure to undo what three college boys attempted to do and could not. I will never forget. Also, if you ever harm Kristina or anyone else, I* will *hunt you down. I* will *scalp you in your sleep. You* will *beg for death.*

Ian Atohi Cameron

Ian put the paper back the way Kristina had left it and closed the refrigerator door with a grin on his face. She might cut his note off before she made the copies to send to the three men and their fathers, but then again, she might not.

Ian Cameron climbed back into bed with his wife and drifted back to sleep, dreaming of a mother bear and her mate walking on the mountain with their playful cubs. It was snowing.

The End

Emily Sharpe

Emily Sharpe is the pen name for a writer, editor and illustrator in south Florida. A former newspaper columnist, she loves to travel and perform in community theater. Mother of four and grandmother of five, Emily substitute teaches, sings, volunteers in the community and attends a raucous group of writers once a month called "Use Your Words." She heartily believes in love and finding one's joy – and she hopes you enjoy this story of romance. Readers may contact her by e-mail: emilysharpebooks@gmail.com.

Don't miss these exciting titles by Emily Sharpe and Blushing Books!

Dear Editor series
Dear Editor
The Stonemason and the Lady
Mating Season

Blushing Books

Blushing Books is one of the oldest eBook publishers on the web. We've been running websites that publish spanking and BDSM related romance and erotica since 1999, and we have been selling eBooks since 2003. We hope you'll check out our hundreds of offerings at http://www.blushingbooks.com.

Blushing Books Newsletter

Please join the Blushing Books newsletter
to receive updates & special promotional offers.
You can also join by using your mobile phone:
Just text **BLUSHING** to 22828.